FORSAKEN CITY

BOOK I OF THE IRON SPIRES TRILOGY

BY LIAM ULLAND-JOY

To Lesley,
Thanks for buying my book.
Enjoy!   Liam Ulland-Joy
8-16-22

BY LIAM ULLAND-JOY

FORSAKEN CITY

BOOK I OF THE IRON SPIRES TRILOGY

Copyright © 2022 by Liam Ulland-Joy

All rights reserved. Published in the United States by Fox Pointe Publishing, LLP. No part of this book may be reproduced in any form or by any electronic or mechanical means, including information storage and retrieval systems, without permission in writing from the publisher.

This is a work of fiction. Names, places, characters, and incidents are either a product of the author's imagination or are used fictitiously. Any resemblance to actual events, places, organizations, or persons, whether living or dead, is entirely coincidental.

www.foxpointepublishing.com/author-liam-ullandjoy

Library of Congress Cataloging-in-Publication Data
Ulland-Joy, Liam, author.
Olson, Sarah, editor.
Town, Scotty, designer.
Hudson, Becca, cover designer.
Forsaken City / Liam Ulland-Joy. – First edition.
Summary: A young Sardourian soldier's unit is sent to infiltrate the heart of Iron Spires, a city occupied by the ruthless Insurrectionists.
ISBN 978-1-952567-38-4 (hardcover) / 978-1-952567-39-1 (softcover)
[1. Military Science Fiction – Fiction. 2. Dystopian – Fiction.
3. Action & Adventure – Fiction.]
Library of Congress Control Number: 2 0 2 2 9 3 4 7 0 7

Printed and bound in the United States of America by Lakeside Press Inc.
First printing July 2022

Dedicated to my family

I

"GOT A VISUAL, ATOLL?" It was Sergeant Greene's muffled snap, the third time I had heard it in the past few minutes.

"Not yet, sir," I responded flatly as I peered through the cold tactical goggles. Digital overlays built into the lenses frantically danced before my eyes, combing the savannah floor in search of our destination. I felt the truck jolt as we picked up speed: a heavy beast of a vehicle, it was intended for troop transport through combat zones, but was now facing a tougher challenge than ever: barreling across the bombed-out roads of Lusira, dodging sniper nests and dipping in and out of friendly territory.

We were accompanied by other vehicles, of course: four other trucks and a speedy light tank which led the procession. Our convoy had long been held up at the border due to electrical issues, and we aimed to make up for our tardiness with superior speed.

Finally, our destination came into view: a collection of squat buildings stretched out across half a mile known as Talon Base. Overhead, a trio of gunships returned from patrol and made a practiced landing at one of the base's several makeshift helipads.

"Got visual, sir!" I shouted. The sergeant grabbed a radio and relayed our arrival to Talon Base. Confirmation trickled back through the comm feed.

The base would only be our first stop. We were to be deployed to Iron Spires, the most notorious and bloody scene of the whole war. Named for the enormous steel skyscrapers and unfeeling metal towers that perforated the city, Iron Spires had a long history in this war, having been forcibly seized by Insurrectionists years ago.

As we arrived, we approached a heavy steel gate and were forced to stop.

"Everyone out!" commanded the sergeant.

In a matter of seconds, the men in every one of our vehicles had extricated themselves and formed up into a single line, dozens long, behind the sergeant. We approached a small yet heavily reinforced concrete box, from which a lone soldier sat dryly demanding identification.

"Atoll, Damien... Private," he eventually said. I approached the box and handed him my small military identification card. The angular blue ID had been noticeably dulled from the typical sheen of standard-issue equipment.

The solider squinted, holding it up to a screen mounted on the wall of his box. After an agonizing pause, he nodded assent and returned it to me. The gate, now open, was freely welcoming a growing stream of my comrades, who I followed dutifully into Talon Base.

I waited as the sergeant directed the rest of my unit into the base and jogged over to join the main group. We were both a sizeable company and experienced... relatively speaking that is. I looked expectantly to the officer as he spoke grimly through the radio. Indistinct voices chattered back. Holstering the device, he gestured for everyone to gather round, his face set in a look of dark acceptance.

"Listen up, Operators," he began, as though to delay the announcement. "Our orders have changed. We're not going into the city as a combined formation."

A few soldiers murmured to one another, but I knew better. Anything louder than the faintest whisper could set the sergeant off. However, he didn't seem to be paying much mind.

The sergeant continued, "I see you're mostly Sardourian, so you probably know...er," he hesitated, "or have heard, that allies in Lusira funneled aid and supplies into their tech centers in Iron Spires and their surrounding country...er. That is," again hesitating. It seemed to me he was trying to gauge just how much information he thought we low-ranked privates would absorb. "Until they lost control of their nearby landholdings and then the city of spires itself." He concluded, "In short, Command is disbanding us."

I felt like I was shriveling up; I began to slouch and lose focus. This was the most catastrophic news I could receive.

"You still paying attention, Atoll?" the sergeant grunted.

"Yessir," I said, snapping to attention. I had been losing focus lately; it was only my second assignment and I was headed for the infamous Iron Spires. And now... without comrades I could depend on.

Throughout my tour in Lusira, I had been comfortable executing the will of the Sardourian government, but it was curious that they would split up a seasoned unit, especially for such a volatile mission.

"We'll be staying at Talon Base overnight and shipping out to Spires in the morning," the sergeant relayed. I barely heard him.

"Each squad-size detachment will consist of twenty soldiers and be under the command of one of my senior officers," Sarge continued. "Command thinks we will work better, faster, and more widely as three separate task forces. So, squad up, bunk down, clean your guns, and, eh, find your might. Dismissed to new formation."

We divided up into three groups, the sergeant directed us to our new team and commanding officer. Everyone started shaking hands to honor our past campaign together, and I followed suit.

Why would three small forces be better than one? While we moved about reorganizing, I recalled what I could of my history lessons at my Construction League training. Sardourian leaders assured the Monarch of their commitment to the pact with Lusira and, within days, a full mobilization had been ordered. Drafts of the Sardourian population were ordered, anticipating stiff resistance from the fighters of the insurrection. The Kabat Vi had already seized a half-dozen major cities and were certainly not inclined to give them up to their hated neighbors. As Sardouria immersed itself in the war, slowly but surely taking over for the Lusirans in frontline engagements against the Insurrectionists, a glaring issue in the Kabat Vi strategy was exposed: their choice to move forward the date of the uprising had led to a disjointed start, with their troops in several cities not equipped to combat the Lusiran forces standing guard. But, if being disjointed was a "glaring issue," why was the 14th Division, my division, being disbanded and reformed? Command must know more than what they taught us in training. After all, in the early stages of the war, ill-prepared Kabat Vi struck with what firepower they possessed.

Through sheer force of will and numerical advantage, they routed the Lusiran military across the nation, forcing them to regroup miles from the cities. We were also told that these initial successes concealed a major weakness in the Kabat Vi's military tactics which their commanders had largely overlooked: without heavy equipment and reinforcements, each city would eventually fall to an overwhelming counterattack. I considered the Sardourian brass must think the Kabat Vi organization was marked for expiry from the moment it was established.

My squad fanned out into a wide semicircle around a squat, leather-faced old officer with a flak helmet snugly nestled on his head and a therm rifle—one of our standard-issue small arms sporting an affixed scope—over his back. Our squad's corporal, I presumed. It was hard to put a name to the face; I hadn't had much experience with this man. After a moment, something clicked: it was Corporal Bridger, who oversaw the largest battles during my first assignment. Conversation broke out amongst the other squads, forming a buzzing background noise as the corporal waited a moment. "It'll be nice to work with you," he continued with a shout as we stood at attention. "Follow me ahead and to the left!" He turned around and walked into Talon Base. With a quick look from the checkpoint guard, the Sardourian guards stepped aside as we entered.

The interior of Talon Base was bustling with activity. As the primary siege base of the Sardourian military outside Iron Spires, it clearly had some perks. I saw a soldier playing accordion to a trio of Lusiran troopers to my left, and far to my right, I could barely see an artillery gun firing rounds towards the city which was some distance outside the base. Groups of military men and women, soldiers and officers alike, hurried in neat lines from one end of the base to another, ripping open tent flaps and clambering inside or pushing open the doors to thin, boxy wood structures built by officers. It seemed to me many here had been trained in the Construction Legion. As Bridger and our squadron made our way down the left side of the base, I continued my distracted reflections from training.

As local Lusiran forces were unable to recapture their home cities, Sardourian shock troops from the mobilization reached the front. Siege tactics were costly and prolonged, for a metropolis such as Iron Spires or the southern stronghold of Kelfort would possess more than enough resources to supply fierce, spartan Kabat Vi occupiers for years. A war of such length was not in the interest of either the Monarch of Lusira or the government of Sardouria, which instead opted for brutal assault tactics, first choking off each city and proceeding to launch brutal, overwhelming assaults against the—admittedly stubborn—Insurrectionists.

Over the years, enthusiastic radio updates made sure to remind the troops this military doctrine would prove relatively successful against the Kabat Vi, as grueling attacks with a central focal point crumbled the resistance and allowed a flow of troops into the city. I was told Sardourian-Lusiran conquerors would liberate the entire area. While this is how most battles played out, some theaters of the war proved memorable—and horrifically bloody—exceptions. A large contingent of thousands of well-fed Kabat Vi escaped Kelfort after nearly a month of fighting in that city. They began terrorizing Sardourian military convoys. Leaving dozens dead in their wake, this threat was extremely difficult to contain without the widespread use of aircraft. The coveted warplanes were always out of reach, however, and we were continually reminded of their vital role in the bombardment of the great city-fortresses.

We reached our apparent destination: a row of dull green military tents, clearly of Lusiran design, which would each fit at least three of us. Bridger declared it mealtime and we broke out our ration packs. Most soldiers stayed outside of the cramped tents, but I wandered in somberly. The interior was sparse: a few bedrolls and a couple dull lanterns. I dropped my pack and sat on a cleanish bedroll with a sigh.

I tore open my bag and bit into a nutrient bar inside. It tasted faintly like an unspecified meat. A sandwich and packaged fruit were also included. I took a sip from my canteen as well; normally, meals were one of the better parts of the day, but on this grim evening, chatter was entirely absent; tactical discussion nonexistent. I was alone with my thoughts.

Would we face the same fate as the stories I heard from teachers at the Construction Legion Academy? My training hadn't been long, but they did give us enough background to know who and what we may be fighting. I knew this much: because of the Kabat Vi column harassing our convoys, a formation of armored vehicles and infantry was assigned to Sardourian Sergeant Greene, who was instructed to fight the Kabat Vi in the manner that they fought—as a counter-guerrilla. The sergeant proved remarkably effective in this way. He anticipated the moves of the Insurrectionists before they were able to strike at the fat, easy targets. This foresight allowed supply columns to begin rolling across the Lusiran countryside in greater numbers. I fought under the sergeant during this campaign. While the concept of sudden lightning raids was exciting, I was an untested private of the

Construction Legion, so I was largely assigned mundane tasks such as repairing or simply guarding the flanks of our armored vehicles.

There were exceptions to this rule, however, which were experiences of the kind that engrave themselves permanently into one's memory. I took part in three raids during that campaign—I remembered them clearly as I took a bite of bitter fruit. Talking was disallowed except when the raid leader was murmuring orders. Even in those cases, the officer in charge spoke in a predetermined set of code phrases designed to minimize verbiage. It went without saying that both flashlights and laser sights were strictly forbidden. When we reached a Kabat Vi camp, we formed up in a circle around it, left a few men back to act as marksmen, then rushed in with automatic therms to gun down the crew of Insurrectionists within a minute. Hours of walking culminated in a single, brutal attack; it was how I expected most of my time in the Sardourian military to play out. Such raids, when mixed with a little repair and fortification work, thanks to my credentials with the mechanic and building courses in my six months at the Construction Legion, grew to become my expectation of life in the war. After unceasing raids on the Kabat Vi camps and utterly hammering their forces, the column of rebels surrendered and the campaign was declared a success.

That was about the time I was made aware of my second military expedition: reassignment to Iron Spires. It was a truly heart-stopping order, but I had, by that point, hardened into a better soldier than I thought possible. I did not shout, complain, or even cry like some of the other Sardourian troopers I witnessed. Rather, I took my position with a sense of resigned duty. How sadly ironic that my second mission could well be my last…

Soldiers, officers, and privates alike spoke of it in grim tones. I heard murmured tales outside my tent. Iron Spires was a dark void on the soil—it sucked in thousands of men and women on all sides of the conflict and never let go until they were mangled flesh on the ground; tired, bloody, changed.

And the city itself? It was the largest city in Lusira, even more so than the capital. It was the epicenter of the Kabat Vi movement. With a population in the millions and a long-standing economic powerhouse fueling its local industry, Iron Spires was considered the greatest testament to Lusiran scientific progress. Ultimately, however, it had been transformed into a hellscape. Other metropolises of the nation may have been "hit hard," but words were simply not enough to describe the devastation that had rocked the city during the River Insurrection. The sheer numbers of Kabat Vi uprisers in the city shocked the defending Lusiran troops, who were overtaken, killed, or forced to flee from the city and abandon their expensive artillery and thermal emplacements to the rebellion. Once a regional hub of science, advanced biotechnology, and learning, Iron Spires became the most staunchly defended stronghold of an interminably stubborn insurgency. I suddenly had no appetite.

I packaged what remained of my rations and looked at my gear. The quiet din of the evening was setting in, and I wondered how I fit into the grand Sardourian scheme. A graduate of the Construction Legion would be valuable in urban warfare, to be sure, but one with such limited experience was surely a risk. Was Command getting desperate?

I had been surprised to learn that Iron Spires was among the first cities pegged for liberation once the great mobilization of Sardouria had taken full effect. A massive disposition of Lusiran and Sardourian coalition troops surrounded the city and laid siege, trying over and over to smash inward. They never made it very far into the interior of the city before being turned back by a tide of ferocious Kabat Vi fighters, appearing out of windows and around corners like great swarms of bats.

Full-frontal assaults caused outrageous casualties among the Sardourians, who suffered terrible conditions during the attacks. A few footholds in the city were gained during the repeat slaughters. The Sardourian populace argued these were not enough to justify the volume of death. The Sardourian government ignored the cries and intensified their efforts to take the city to boot. Paratroopers were dropped in continuous air raids. Lusiran forces made their own attempts to invade the city, but all were beaten back by an absurdly dedicated Kabat Vi defense. It went against all preconceived plans for the progression of the war; strategic doctrine had to be modified to account for the stronghold of Iron Spires remaining in Insurrectionist hands. The city, as a shining economic hub, was a valuable stronghold for the insurrection and it would take only the most vigorous assaults to penetrate. I sat on a cot and rubbed my tired eyes. It seemed the fighting was weighing heavily on my mind.

One bright thread I could grasp on to was that the militaries of the two nations had succeeded in recapturing most cities from the insurrection in recent months. These operations reduced the presence of the Kabat Vi in these urban centers to a mere low-level resistance.

I raised my head as low conversation cut through the canvas tent and my reflections. "Jasper, Splint, Rodney, you three go form up with the base patrols and make yourselves useful!" instructed Bridger. I could hear them quietly stowing what remained of their ration packs and trotting away back towards the center of Talon Base. "The rest of you, get into those tents and stay in 'em!" he spat at the remainder of the squad. Two men pushed through the flaps of my tent. They nodded at me silently.

Neither they nor I seemed intent on conversation, and I barely recognized them anyways. I spent much of this available time cleaning out my therm rifle. It had been known to get clogged with dust at the worst times.

Despite the occasional jam, I was most familiar with this weapon, and it had served me well over the course of my previous campaign; it was a reliable, mass-produced gunmetal steel weapon with a slot for a stored therm magazine behind the active one. In time, I had learned shorthand ways to operate the weapon. It was built with a small switch on the underside for instant release of the primary magazine in an emergency. I could grab onto the mag while holding down the switch to slip out the magazine more quickly.

I pondered my assignment once more: Iron Spires was the most lethal assignment one could be given in this war. I had it good with my guerrilla assignment. Clearly, fate had made the choice—without my consideration—to balance out my luck. After obsessively cleaning my therm rifle, I finally conceded that I had probably annihilated almost every speck of dust across the whole body of the metallic gun. I packed up my equipment and lay down to rest, trying my best to avoid thinking of the great maw that was Iron Spires.

I drifted off to the sound of our artillery cracking off shots towards the city.

In my dream, I was back in Sardouria. It was much different from the endless plains, hills, and forests of this country; Sardouria was more than that. It was a paradise. Every landscape was picturesque. So vivid you could swear it wasn't formed but painted from the colors of soil and grass. Everything, right down to the smell of the earth, was different. I saw the tree-covered mountains of my hometown, but something was different. I blinked in my dream, not once, but twice, and whipped around. I was sinking. The pristine cottages of the Sardourian village began to rise up all around and swallow my miniscule self. As I thrashed and resisted, a single thought permeated my mind: I was being buried.

I was brusquely shaken awake by one of my comrades, who had a hurried expression on his face. "Get up, soldier! The base is hit!"

I scrambled to my feet and burst through the tent flaps awkwardly. One of my arms still fought to find the correct sleeve in my armor. I spun around as the crisp morning air washed over me and I looked for the impact crater. A column of smoke rose from the center of the base. Alarms blared frantically as Sardourians and Lusirans alike rushed to the scene with a heavy hose built into a nearby electric water well. As I approached the growing crowd, I noticed in horror as shattered figures were lifted from the smoky debris. Several of the boxy wooden rooms had exploded, the shrapnel and wreckage was everywhere within a forty-foot circle, and the ground was thoroughly charred, the dark oranges and browns of the exposed soil now smeared with ash.

"One..." A pause, then... "...two dead!" shouted a grave Lusiran trooper. A couple of grunts carried away the bodies on stretchers. I saw Corporal Bridger near the scene, talking loudly with another Sardourian officer. "ID?" I heard him shout. I trotted towards him, just in time to hear the other officer respond: "Didn't get a good look at them. Talk to the carriers," he said, referring to the soldiers who lifted the bodies from the area.

Other officers were screaming orders as neat rows of Sardourian and Lusiran troops took up positions at the defenses around the base and secured the perimeter. "What happened?" I shouted to Bridger as I came into range, "I graduated from the Construction Legion. I can help with repairs..."

Bridger's face was inscrutable; he may have been trying to size me up. "Kabat Vi, of course..." he said gruffly, "And you refer to me as 'Sir' when speaking to me."

I nodded firmly, "Yes, sir."

"They've got a gun position in uptown," Bridger continued, "and a load of rockets came up, overwhelming our anti-air systems." To illustrate this, he pointed to a cluster of mechanized turrets in the distance, each armed with four automatic cannons.

"There's two more hits right outside the base," he added. Despite his coarse voice, his words were clear as cut glass in a brand-new therm rifle long-scope. "Let the seasoned engineers clean up this mess, Atoll." Soldiers continued to rush around. Bridger continued, "This doesn't change anything. We're still heading into Spires this morning." As he turned away, he held a radio to his mouth, but a body carrier hurriedly approached and cut the corporal off. "Sir!" the grunt shouted, before whispering something to Bridger. As they spoke, I noticed that these body carriers were equipped with heavier, shock-resistance combat armor. Bridger shuddered almost imperceptibly.

"Get me J4 from the Bombardiers, II Squad," he ordered.

"Yessir," the carrier said, turning on his heel and rushing away.

The carnage of the situation continued as the fires finally subsided. Corporal Bridger approached me again.

"One of the dead was Specialist Rodney." he said matter-of-factly. "We'll need someone to replace him as he was an invaluable recon man. I've 'requested' an old comrade, J4. Won't be a problem, will it?" he asked. Obviously a rhetorical question, Bridger marched off to coordinate with our other men, who had simply amassed at the edge of the crater and idled there. I followed him just in time to hear that we were ordered back to our tents to make final preparations. We were rolling out now.

Sirens pierced the morning air as dozens of soldiers sprinted back and forth. I returned to the tent and grabbed the last bits of equipment I had left strewn around. The other soldiers of the Special Operators were collected outside the tents, with more emerging until finally, all twenty of us were assembled.

"Don't let the rocket strikes fool you, Operators. The local Insurrection is on its last legs. Their last bastion is downtown, with only pockets in other areas. Our job is to ensure the total collapse of the Insurrection in the city. We will be smashing through their border defenses with an armored convoy and making our way downtown. At which point, we will link up with Sardourian reinforcements and take command of the area to coordinate..." Bridger clicked his tongue thoughtfully, "an effective assault on the remaining Insurrectionists in the area."

He walked up and down our lines, studying us intently. "We represent justice, ladies and gentlemen. Do this unit proud... do not even think about..." he trailed off, the first time I heard him do so. "Any questions?" he demanded.

There were no questions from the unit—the corporal was met with stony silence. It was a lot to take in. The way he described it, we stood a fighting chance against the hardened Insurrectionist defenders. I wasn't sure whether to believe him or not.

We drew our weapons, divided up into two lines, and followed him to the far left end of the base. Four armored vehicles were waiting, each with a therm mounted on top. Loaded with equipment inside, these fighting vehicles were cramped, squat, and tough enough to resist a barrage of small-arms fire. Corporal Bridger directed us from vehicle to vehicle, five men to a car. I climbed into the back left seat of the vehicle that was second from the front and opened the window to fire my therm. A strange man I'd never seen before climbed in after me. He was decked out in several secured medals but sporting standard-issue flak armor. He wore no helmet but I noticed a single bright green light flickered from the peculiar metal chip over his eyebrow. It blinked every ten seconds or so. I tried not to stare, but the man turned to face me nonetheless.

"J4," he said. "They call me Jan." He extended his hand and I took it. J4... the one sent to replace the late Specialist Rodney.

"I didn't mean to stare... I just..." I tried to say. A few clipped laughs made their way out of Jan's mouth. His tight facial expression and longer hair belied his experience.

"Never seen one, eh?" he asked. I was stunned.

"So you're an augment?"

"Yes, sir," Jan responded with a possible hint of sarcasm. I knew he outranked me; his patch suggested he was a Specialist. I wondered what his implant did—some augments never told anyone. If I had to guess, it likely heightened an attribute which would prove valuable in combat. I had heard stories of augs with superior strength, reflexes, or agility from my comrades, but meeting one in person had left me inexplicably speechless.

Radio chatter flared up through Jan's radio.

"We're moving!" Bridger's voice instructed. The vehicle rolled forward on command, its heavy frame barreling across the Lusiran road. Through the window behind Jan, I saw the muzzle flares from a half-dozen Sardourian artillery guns in the base firing repeatedly. They were likely supposed to cover our advance towards the city. The cover-fire provided a moment of reassurance until I began to analyze the tactic more logically. Considering how inaccurate the Kabat Vi fire on our base was, the shells from our guns were sure to hit the bombed-out world of Iron Spires with minimal accuracy, having almost no chance of striking an actual Insurrectionist target.

Our convoy picked up speed. Clearly, we thought a breakneck pace could deter any ambushes along the road to Iron Spires.

I sat in tense silence, peering out across the devastated hills of Lusira as the wind whipped across my face through the open window. We hit several bumps along the way, but thankfully mines were not a threat. The Construction Legion had long since cleared this road. On the off chance a new patrol of Insurrectionists had mined the area, hopefully our speed could propel us over the bomb instead of it detonating while we were right on top of it. As our ensemble progressed, various wishes of good luck came through the radio from the troops at Talon Base.

I turned back to Jan, who had a most serious expression on his face as he surveyed the land around us. One of his hands gripped a therm just below his seat. Likely always the recon man.

It wasn't long before the metropolis of Iron Spires itself came into view. It started as a small collection of skyscrapers in the distance but grew exponentially until we could make out the finest details of the damage to the great city. Great gashes had torn apart buildings of all sizes and heights, and pillars of flame and smoke roiled on in multiple areas. The looming monoliths of steel and rust cast great shadows over the soil of Lusira. The sight of explosions going off was jarring, and I watched as the side of an apartment building was vaporized by a rocket. Only the roar of engines and radio chatter broke through the deafening silence among our convoy.

I turned back to Jan, hoping to say something, anything, to cut through the overpowering apprehension that was gnawing at me as we approached Iron Spires. I tried to break the silence. A rocket slammed. With a lurch, we powered through the burst of opaque smoke cloud on the road. Therm fire broke out as we spotted multiple Insurrectionists lying prone in the underbrush and laying down a barrage of heavy flak. Therms didn't make heavy booms or cracks, but rather understated popping sounds as they released a barrage of vicious, flesh-melting rounds towards the enemy.

Thermal rounds were nasty inventions; thin, pointed projectiles that narrowed to a deadly point and could travel with unparalleled velocity. Since their invention in the pre-war days, they rapidly became the weapon of choice. A therm round could dig into your flesh and burn it.

The bullets rang in my ears as they deflected violently off the reinforced steel hull of our transport.

"Counterfire!" shouted Jan, raising his own therm out the open window and returning fire. Our vehicle-mounted guns and soldiers inside engaged the ambushers, but their position in the underbrush was exceedingly hard to hit. We sped on and left them in the dust and smoke clouds instead of finishing them off. Corporal Bridger's orders were to keep going until we hit the city. Several more rockets whizzed by us—one literally flew past my face out the window, and I pulled myself completely back into the vehicle as an outbreak of therm fire followed.

"Suppress the ambush!" Jan repeated several times... I'm trying, I thought. Using my own therm, I fired at a rocketeer who was forced to support himself on a knee as he shot his weapon. My rounds flew harmlessly by them. Why even fire with these conditions? The gunfire stopped as we left the range of the last of the ambushers. Each driver called in on the radio channel to report no casualties.

We were almost at the city border now—out the window, I could see the road into Iron Spires was heavily blockaded. Crude barricades of spikes, wires, and blocks blocked our entry. It would take hours to bypass. Two wooden cupolas, clearly meant to house guards, were located on either side of the barricade.

"Pursuers!" came Jan's voice as I whipped my head around. My heart sank as I saw dozens of Insurrectionists on motorcycles in hot pursuit of our convoy. They fired haphazard potshots with therms and screamed bloody murder. As they closed in, I saw they were clad in an amalgam of dusty jackets, civilian clothes, and rags. Several even wore flak helmets.

Their assault was discombobulated, without a clear leader or formation, but it didn't matter; the firepower spoke for itself. Their rounds cracked past me with harrowing accuracy, several impacting just around my head against the vehicle's interior. My heart dropped into my stomach as I pulled back from the window once more. The inner-vehicle was getting warm. If the truck took too many hits, it would cook us inside. Orders from Bridger came through the radio: we'd have to go off-road and around the barricade.

At the last second, we swerved into a ditch and rattled our way around the heavy barricade. Clearly, this place was meant to be guarded, but the Insurrectionists had all left their posts to ambush us. As the motorcyclists approached, we became aware that we had breached the city limit. We picked up speed, engaging our pursuers with our car-mounted therms. Rounds flew everywhere until, suddenly, a burst of light and heat overwhelmed me, and everything went black.

II

I WAS PULLED OUT OF THE WRECKED VEHICLE BY JAN. My head was spinning. I thought the gunfire had stopped, but it was just being drowned out by the ringing in my ears. Gasping for air, I stumbled to my feet and saw our troops as they jumped from the fiery vehicles and traded therm fire with Insurrectionists. I shook my head, found my therm under a footboard of the armored vehicle, and quickly checked that it wasn't jammed. Bleary-eyed, I took aim. We shot several off their motorcycles who went careening into the debris. I braced myself against the damaged car and tried to get my bearings as I watched Jan pull the driver out of our vehicle and lay him prone beside a tire.

Our men took cover behind the barricade and the piles of rubble, fiercely barraging the tide of Insurrectionists. When one magazine was expended, it was replaced in seconds with practiced efficiency. As the Kabat Vi approached, their formation loosened even more as we downed several more of the motorcycles. Their counterfire weakened. Within minutes, my comrades of the Special Operators successfully suppressed the ambush force. I saw Corporal Bridger at the barricade, studying the road with binoculars. I found Jan pulling corpses out from our wrecked cars. Bridger marched over.

"Report?" he asked. Jan turned and grimly responded, laying down a broken corpse loaded with shrapnel.

"Nota and Ridgewell KIA," he said. "Three injuries."

Everyone pulled back from the barricades. The wounded were laid out on the ground as Bridger oversaw a man with a medic patch who attended to their treatment. I had seen this medic often on my first campaign. His name was Splint. He pulled out what shrapnel he could before cleaning and bandaging the wounds. I saw Private Sitter, an old acquaintance of mine, prone and in pain. He suffered a serious wound from a piece of shrapnel to the leg. We would need a safe location to treat wounds this severe. My dizziness subsided and I lurched my way over to Bridger who gestured for the squad to form up. Everyone assembled in front of Bridger except Splint, who was quietly securing the dead in reinforced bags for later recovery.

"We're inside," Bridger said gravely. As if on cue, a smattering of gunfire and explosions went off in the distance. Fighting was intensifying in other parts of the city.

"Remember our goal," he went on. "Once we make it downtown, we could help end this entire battle. We need to eradicate every last semblance of the resistance in this metallic city."

I nodded, trying to tune out the shock and chaos around me as I shifted my grip on my therm.

"Splint, you almost done?" Bridger called.

"I need Tuna's help!" the medic shouted back. Tuna, a wiry trooper who always seemed to keep his wits about him, looked surprised for a moment before trotting over. Together, they carried a body bag and hid it carefully from view before they regrouped with the squad.

"Time is of the essence, as you well know. The window of opportunity to seize downtown could close at any moment," Bridger paused. "That clear?" he added.

"Yes, sir!" responded the Special Operators, my voice among them. Bridger took point, leading the squad from the area. The background noise of intermittent gunfire and explosions was a pervasive soundtrack to our new scenery. We crept along the edge of a street as the concrete skyscrapers and buildings loomed on either side. Great fallen chunks of their massive structures had piled on the ground in charred mounds. Clouds sagged over the city as if to shield the rest of the world from it.

We took occasional, short breaks inside crumbling shelters to let encroaching gunfire subside before we continued down the street edge. I tried to keep my thoughts attuned—focusing on the here and now, maintaining my weapon, staying aware of the sounds of battle, and keeping up with the soldier in front of me. I tried not to think of the sheer quantity of perfect hiding places for a Kabat Vi Insurrectionist around here. Every manhole, crater, pile of rubble, or window could conceal a hostile. Gusts of chilling wind shivered through the dead city, uncaring of what it touched or whose side you were on.

After almost an hour of tense walking in relative silence, Jan, who was walking behind Bridger, pulled him back. Our line came to a disjointed halt.

"Anti-personnel mines in the street ahead, sir," Jan said. Bridger thought for a moment before turning back to look at the squad.

"Engineers, move up!" he ordered amid a nearby outburst of shell fire.

I and the others, identified by patches as Construction Legion, made our way to the front of the line. I was followed by Tuna. Tuna seemed to be in good spirits despite his recent experience helping Splint with the deceased.

"Broom mines," Tuna nodded knowingly. "Those things can sweep out a whole squad if we're not careful. That magnetocore tech is strong despite its age." Tuna grabbed the handles of two large metal devices each with a flat head like that of a large workshop broom from back home in Sardouria. He handed one to me. Although my training had been more of a "crash course," they took care to cover at least these instruments. I turned it on and held it out in front of me. It clicked over and over at an increasing rate until it emitted a harsh buzz. I steadied my hands but hesitated.

"Now dig it up, man!" Tuna said with a slight grin. I used my one-handed ax to pry up the blacktop and quickly found a dormant mine embedded in the earth below. Named broom mines for their wide tops that spread the blast radius and shrapnel to a maximum distance, these were truly lethal traps used to great effect by the Insurrectionists. All of us engineers set about disabling and digging up the broom mines before tossing them into a pile at the side of the road. It took about half an hour—we were lucky not to have been discovered by any Kabat Vi during that time.

During this time, Bridger organized patrols of the adjacent blocks which would alert us if any Insurrectionists got too close. By the time we had cleared the entire stretch of road, he decided that we needed somewhere to take cover and get our bearings. We had made good time but needed somewhere unexposed to continue treatment of our men and plan our next move.

Tuna and another man lifted Private Sitter and threw each of his arms over their shoulders. We continued along the edge of the concrete-and-glass building, a light haze setting in all around us. The squad made several turns until coming onto a wide street littered with wrecked vehicles and pockmarked with craters. A bombed-out city park bordered the left side of the road while huge, shattered storefronts lined the right side. Bridger called us back around the corner and sent Jan to scout ahead. Jan took cover behind one of the destroyed vehicles and surveyed the area while we peeked apprehensively to see what was going on. He spent several minutes sizing up the scene, even tapping his implant a few times. He returned, hunched over and running, to our position.

"There is a Kabat Vi soldier overlooking the street with a grenade launcher from the rooftop of that parking garage," he said, pointing to a huge concrete structure at the far end of the road.

"Thank you, Jan," Bridger replied before turning to another soldier, a sniper named Orange. She had been an active counter-guerrilla in almost every raid in my first campaign.

"You think you can take him out from here?" he asked Orange.

She thought for a moment before replying, "The wind is too intense, sir, and if I miss, he has a great straight angle on us."

"Any other ideas?"

"See that store there?" she replied, pointing to a department store with an obliterated storefront.

"If we can get to it, lock and load, and mount an assault from there, the wind plays against him, not us. Plus, he won't expect a threat from so close."

Bridger pondered this—clearly, he favored the full-frontal approach to this problem, but he probably needed Orange's tactical consideration.

"Let's be real sneaky then," he said as he gestured for the squad to follow.

I was beginning to admire Bridger. I could see he always took point, never willing to hide behind his own men or send them ahead into something he wouldn't face first. We crouched low and practically waddled to the other side of the street, hugging the shadowed storefronts as we made our way to the department store. Though I couldn't see the Kabat Vi soldier himself, I could see the location where he was perched. The parking garage seemed like an apt location to maintain an overwatch of the entire area. Clearly, Jan had used his implant to make out the details that I couldn't.

In sweaty silence, we filed into the crater that was once the department store lobby and steeled ourselves. Jan raised his heavy therm, Orange her sniper rifle, and Bridger led with his therm. Splint took up the rear, but I noticed the dubious quality of his therm rifle; he clearly made little effort to clean it beyond the bare minimum. We rushed out into the street—I was towards the back of the group. Raising my therm, I quickly found the Kabat Vi soldier through my scope by following the stream of rounds my squad fired. I only had time to fire a couple of my own before the Kabat Vi loosed a grenade from his launcher. It streaked overhead and exploded with a heavy blast behind us, wiping out a section of another concrete store as we attacked. Our intense fire forced him to pull back from the edge, but we knew he was still active up there. Orange stopped behind a wrecked car and sighted the area with her sniper rifle while the rest of us kept our therms pointed at the roof. A thought occurred to me. Why didn't we just use Orange's stealthy snipe instead of this barrage? But it wasn't my place to question Bridger. Gunfire seemed to fall away as I focused on the threat at hand. My trigger finger twitched dangerously. The Insurrectionist had evaded us. His head cropped up behind a parked car in one of the levels of the parking garage as he sent another grenade lancing towards us. We scattered as it exploded viciously against the pavement. Bits of concrete flew everywhere. A few of them sliced into my leg, and I howled with agony as I lurched forward. After a moment, we trained fire on him again, but he ducked down at the last second. We closed in, and I felt the thumping swell of adrenaline coursing in my every step. I was almost to Bridger at the head of the squad when the Insurrectionist appeared a third time. He charged out from a ramp leading into the parking garage. As the mad man sprinted, he fired off a grenade but clearly wasn't even trying to aim—it arched into the sky and slammed into a nearby high-rise, blowing out a dozen windows. However, he had exposed himself by going on the offensive. Our therm rounds pounded into him and he was eventually finished off by an accurate shot from Orange, who was positioned behind us at a destroyed car.

"Wounded!" I shouted as we moved forward into the parking garage. Tuna and another man fanned out to guard our left flank, facing the burnt city park as Orange hurried to link up with the rest of the squad. Splint hurried to me.

"Where are you hit?" he demanded to know.

"The leg... got cut up by shrapnel," I explained with bated breath. With Splint's help, I walked slowly up the ramp with the last of the squad. I saw someone else had confiscated the Insurrectionist's grenade launcher along the way.

"We'll pause here to tend to our wounded," Bridger said, ordering another four soldiers up the parking garage to clear floors of any remaining Kabat Vi. "Atoll and Sitter, sit down!" he demanded.

Sitter looked pallid as he was gingerly helped down. Splint picked most of the shrapnel out of my leg and quickly bandaged it. Then, he focused most of his attention on the ailing Sitter. Splint looked frustrated as he dug through his medical bag. I heard him relay to Bridger that he didn't have the right chem for such an "insidious" infection. Sitter agonizingly moaned and then eventually screamed. I knew he succumbed when, finally, he went absolutely silent.

Splint stood up with a hard look on his face, then demanded to know, "What's our plan? We're gonna keep losing men, Corporal." Tuna quietly opened another body bag from the inventory and tended Sitter's limp corpse. His grin was unequivocally gone.

"We'll camp here for the night…" repeated Corporal Bridger slowly, directed at Splint. He continued to the rest of us, "It's only open to fire from an elevated position and the ramp is a perfect bottleneck." Bridger assigned guard positions and announced the regime.

"Adir, Tuna, LaReye… mount a therm at the top of that ramp. In our current condition, we can't advance in darkness. We're digging in here, and we're not leaving until the light shines again."

"Sir, yes, sir," they responded rigidly.

The sounds of battle throughout the city were relentless—in fact, the night air seemed to amplify them. I sat crouched in the parking garage with only a few of our dimmed solar lanterns casting a sickly yellow hue. The pain in my leg subsided, but I knew it would be quite some time before I'd be able to sleep in this landscape of death. I sat in silence until Jan approached me to relay that I was to man the therm at the top of the ramp in a few hours, so I should try to sleep. I reluctantly complied, withdrawing a sleeping bag from my pack, but I kept my eyes open to watch our guards. Tuna and Splint were at the walls while two others, who I couldn't identify in the dark, sat talking under their breath at the top of the ramp where the mounted therm sat idle. The rest of the squad was arrayed in a circle with each member either in a sleeping bag or sitting and cleaning a weapon. I watched as Jan dumped out a bag of ammunition; it held a few dozen cartridges of therm ammunition to power us through our offensive. These magazines, each containing thirty therm rounds, could be inserted modularly, either into the bottom or side of the rifles for convenience in battle.

The wind was as incessant as the sounds of gunfire. As I drifted, it seemed to me that Iron Spires was a biodome of death; a perfect natural environment for bloody, endless combat.

I don't know at what moment I knew I was dreaming, but I felt light as my mind lingered on my hometown in Sardouria—away from Iron Spires, away from the Insurrectionists, away from the blood and screaming. Inescapably, I was brought back and dragged across the dreamland border into this other world; this other war...

Jan woke me up. Tuna was behind him, evidently waiting to take my place. He looked extraordinarily tired, holding his therm loosely and slouching a bit in the dark morning air. Some sounds of battle persisted, but diminished, a lull in the night. For that, I was grateful. I groaned as I got to my feet, picked up my rifle, and headed to the top of the ramp. I switched places with a guard who had been sitting at the tripod-mounted therm. I sat down and put both hands on the handles of the gun, getting a feel of the weight and power of the weapon. It was a heavy flak weapon that had been assembled by another engineer. Jan joined me after a few seconds. He squatted next to me with something in his hands.

"Darklens," he said, handing one to me. "Did you think we'd ask you to shoot into the shadows?" he asked with a slight hint of amusement. I fumbled with the device, having never seen one before. Even during the night raids of my first campaign, we hadn't been afforded access to this kind of technology; clearly our operations here were granted a higher priority by the Sardourian brass. I noted that Jan didn't wear a darklens. His implants must have provided the same effect.

I clipped the darklens to the rim of my helmet and peered through it. It provided decent night-vision, but it would short out at random moments. I didn't know how long, if at all, the battery would last. The wind whispered through the old parking garage again as I surveyed the city around me. The parking ramp sloped down until it met a fork in the road. Turning right would take you back down the wide street we had assaulted this building from, but going straight would eventually get you to a left turn that would take you further into the city. I maintained a line of fire across this street for what felt like only minutes. It was surely hours, though, as I soon witnessed the black sky turn to a light gray out of the corner of my eye.

I yawned, took both hands off the mounted therm, and straightened my helmet. Morning was coming soon. I occupied myself with thoughts of home; my family had approved of my decision to enter the military, saying I would be offering a great service to the citizens of not one, but two countries. Before I enlisted in the Construction Legion, I worked as a builder, helping make the foundations of little houses and cottages in Sardouria proper. As a graduate of the Sardourian National Trade Academy and with my subsequent work experience, Construction Legion was the best fit for my skill set. I felt a growing ache for the simpler days building homes.

A therm round smashed into the concrete at my feet with a jarring crack and I was lurched from my thoughts. The shot triggered a glare in my darklens and sent a wave of blinding light straight into my retina. I tore off the darklens and refocused my spotted vision to the street below. I spun my head around and saw them up at the left turn. A group of Kabat Vi were advancing on the parking garage. They were well-armed with heavy therms and stolen flak armor. The dull morning muted the red of the flying eagle sigil each of the Insurrectionists displayed somewhere on their person.

"Hostiles! Hostiles!" shouted Jan, who had dropped the ammo bag he was studying to awaken the rest of our men.

The Insurrectionists' therm rounds raced through the air towards Jan and me—instinct bubbled and I released the safety of the mounted therm. We blasted heated rounds through the air at an incredible rate. The stream forced the Kabat Vi to take cover in the wreckage of the street. The enemy continued their charge, however, and laid down cover fire for the assault. I knew I was toast if I stayed still. I made an executive decision and heaved the therm up out of its tripod, hauling it around to the concrete wall of the parking garage to set it up there. Therm rounds chased me the whole way, but Jan's cover fire seemed to prevent the entire barrage from coming my way. A few therm rounds collided in midair, creating a violent fireball.

Our troops had rushed to their feet and were scrambling to set up a line of defense. I could only pray the enemy didn't have explosive weapons. A well-placed grenade would produce a horrific mess of shrapnel in such close quarters.

I continued to lay down withering fire, but they moved in short bursts between cover and reloads. My focus was constantly being divided and subverted. I couldn't get a shot at these scumbags. What good was all this firepower if everyone was behind cover?

Behind me, I was vaguely aware of Orange shouting something to Bridger. He roared assent. I had no time to turn around and see what was going on; the Kabat Vi were closing the distance quickly.

From what I could see, there were about fifteen of them, all decked out with the same dull maroon headbands and bandana-like fabric. This was a cohesive attack team, and they were weaseling their way up to our position. I turned the gun as best I could to suppress their counterattack. Our rifle fire was meeting only limited success as the hail of bullets impacted against the cracked and battered obstacles. The barrage was tearing through ammunition and we didn't have much to show for it.

I abandoned the heavy therm altogether and took aim with my longer, more accurate rifle.

My heat rounds whipped through the morning air; one, then two rounds smashed into the Kabat Vi forces. My first shot tore apart the shoulder ligaments of an Insurrectionist assaulter, while the second nearly vaporized a Kabat Vi's unarmored head. In an instant, I mentally processed what I had done and moved on. I doubted the Insurrectionists would be so kind as to give me such a quick death once they reached our lines. My sense of duty was underpinned by my growing terror. I bit my lip and continued to fire searing thermal rounds.

As the attackers grew closer, the accuracy of my squad only improved.

A ringing blast from somewhere above caused my heart to pound. The Construction Legion Academy trained us to stabilize our mental acuity so we would falter less, but I never mastered the skill. One of the approaching Kabat Vi dropped dead instantly before me, shot through the skull by a high-powered thermal round. I looked up.

Orange! She had set up a position above us and had the high ground on the Insurrectionists.

As if summoned, several more Kabat Vi with similar headbands and bandanas appeared in open windowsills overlooking the street. They raised their therms and sent a storm of rounds towards the second level, trying to suppress Orange.

Alarmed, I forced myself to point my rifle away from the rapidly closing Insurrectionists and fired quick, well-aimed shots at the Kabat Vi positioned at the windows. Above me, the sound of Orange's sniper rifle stopped and I saw no more silhouetted figures in the windows. Meanwhile, more than a dozen Kabat Vi were less than thirty feet from the ramp. A second's respite in the gunfire allowed me to reload, but they suddenly launched a full-scale charge. A grenade sailed overhead, ricocheted off the concrete floor of the parking garage, and exploded in a burst of flame. Someone was screaming and burning behind me as the Insurrectionists closed on us. I heard Splint roaring for the blazing soldier to stop running around. In a few seconds, I gunned down several more—the rest dove for cover, but their momentum had been quelled. We continued to trade smattered fire until only four Kabat Vi remained. Their fire quieted as they tucked in cover.

Bridger called out suddenly, "Hold Fire!"

We held. The near silence was alarming and I could feel the pulse among our squad as exacerbated breaths filled the void.

They came out from their positions with hands over their heads, brows furrowed and despondent. We raised our rifles as they approached to be sure they didn't try any tricks.

"Get on your knees!" Bridger commanded. They took slow steps forward.

He added, "Down to the ground! Get down!"

I realized I was holding my breath.

They twisted suddenly and revealed pistols in each of their hands. They fired off several therm rounds before we shot them down. Corporal Bridger himself landed the final shots on two of them. He jogged down the ramp, kicked the pistols from the prone bodies, and checked pulses on each. Jan and Splint did the same to the other deceased.

"Status?" Bridger demanded.

"Kanto burned alive." Splint said with frustrated rage. He added, "Some others have therm wounds... sir, we've gotta change our strategy here. We're too static."

Bridger waved him off, "Splint, our tactics are sound; these guys look like augments. Not our fault if we face the most elite of the Kabat forces on our second day here."

I joined them... The figures indeed appeared to be augments. Various implants stuck out of their head and arms. I noted a line of wires running down the forearm of one, while another had some kind of cybernetic visor.

Jan looked askance at the corpses, with a clear note of disgust in his voice when he said, "They don't deserve to be."

Splint rolled his eyes and returned to the rest of the troops. He helped some get their bearings and tended others' wounds. I stood with Bridger and Jan at the base of the ramp as we watched the sky morph from a dull blue to warm, buttery yellows and oranges which reflected off the glass debris littered chaotically around the street.

"They'll be sending another force to investigate the sounds of battle," Jan said. "Continuous gunfire is different from a skirmish, it warrants more attention from the Insurrectionists. Over the past two years, intel has suggested that Kabat Vi don't react passively when they lose track of an attack force. They will almost surely be dispatching a unit with three men for every one in this group."

"Wise counsel as always," Bridger grunted, his words carrying a tone of tired appreciation. "We should be moving out."

Jan stayed at the foot of the ramp while Bridger and I returned to the chaotic scene in the parking garage. Orange returned from her perch on the second level in time to see Splint desperately attempting to resuscitate another soldier. The medic's intense labors finally caused the man to spasm with hacking coughs before sputtering to life, exhausted and thoroughly shaken. The other soldiers hurriedly cleaned their therms and armor, tended to their injuries, and checked bandages. Splint was actively commanding some of the troops while Bridger issued orders to others. Everyone gathered their supplies, packed sleeping bags, and stowed magazines of therm ammunition. The scene was more chaotic than the Corporal probably would have liked, but at least we were moving.

One thing was sure though—morale was low. The surprise attack had left many more of us wounded and downtrodden.

Splint ordered some men to watch our perimeter while Bridger ordered the others to pack up and head out. After about five minutes, everything was sorted and the bleary-eyed troops were ready to move again. Admittedly, it was sooner than we expected, but no one complained...yet.

Bridger was distant as we formed a ragtag procession, making our way down the ramp and onto the street before, picking our way through the wreckage and corpses until we approached the left turn. As we carried on, he scanned the area for threats but did not often redirect our movements. I could practically feel Splint's seething rage from my position. The usual orchestra of battle was forming the soundscape of Iron Spires for the day once again, with rockets and grenades exploding somewhere deeper in the city punctuated by the staccato chatter of therm fire.

We persevered doggedly through the city in a loose formation. As we traveled, I noticed that Splint had taken stride right behind Bridger. That was usually Jan's position. Splint was getting bold.

Over time, our options for movement became more restricted. Whole blocks were completely mined, areas were barricaded and wired up, and there were even places submerged underwater or crammed with destroyed vehicles. The foreboding pillars of the Iron Spires skyscrapers towered above us, uncaring of our plight. We spent much of the morning dodging small groups of Insurrectionists, taking refuge in hidey-holes, and stopping to replace bandages.

One time, I spotted a lone Sardourian soldier on a distant rooftop; he was just a speck, but I picked him out with the scope of my rifle. He was alone and fighting off a wave of Insurrectionists. I watched him take out one, then two with his therm before being overwhelmed.

It was a sobering sight and it forced us to find shelter immediately. With that kind of Kabat Vi activity in the area, it would be good to get to a more secluded location for a while. Bridger ordered a two-hour break after spotting what appeared to be a slightly damaged bunkhouse on the edge of a wide street. The bunkhouse was unremarkable and spanned the alleyway between two similarly large urban buildings. In fact, its primary trait was that it might even have been less damaged than most structures in the area.

Bridger led the way into the bunkhouse followed by Splint, Jan, Tuna, me, then the others. Our troops swept the whole building, eventually concluding that the greatest threat to the security of the unit was a nasty film of dust that seemed to coat the entire structure. Nothing was left untouched by the thick coat—the building was almost a museum, a testament to the pre-war Iron Spires. Almost everything had been perfectly preserved after its tenants abandoned it, save for a single hole in the topmost floor, clearly bashed open by a flying piece of debris in a Lusiran bombing.

We laid claim to our day's territory, hurrying to harvest what useful materials we could scavenge. Orange set up in one of the upstairs rooms, looking out over an expansive parking lot.

Our new command center certainly wasn't perfect. For instance, we could only overlook one angle of the city: straight out towards the parking lot. Splint was visibly fuming at this, calling it another static and dangerous choice for making camp. It was a testament to his sway in the unit that Bridger didn't arrest him right there. I saw the slovenly way soldiers responded to Bridger followed by Splint's lurking check-ins with each one. Splint had to know what he was doing and the threat his actions posed to our cohesion, but I had no room to interfere. Just earlier today, I had blown a soldier's head wide open and was still trying to slow the tremor I felt in my palms. Refocused, I smashed the window next to the fine mahogany front door and maintained a solid line of fire across the parking lot with my therm rifle. Nothing out of the ordinary. My ears attuned to my comrades behind me. I heard lingering complaints, which hushed only when Bridger grew near. Tuna tried to make jokes to keep the soldiers' spirits up, but his joviality sounded more forced each time. A few of us didn't complain no matter the circumstance: Jan was fiercely loyal, Orange was the stoic sniper who rarely held prolonged conversations, and I was too busy taking in everything and trying to get my own thoughts under control to complain. The overpowering sense of terror had been ever-present, and I was sure it had dealt an equally painful strike against the morale of the others. I pretended not to be listening, but I could hear the breathy whispers of possible changes. "Splint" and "Bridger" were popular mentions from what I could hear. An hour passed. I kept a close watch on the parking lot.

"How're you doing, Atoll?" It was Bridger. Ah, I wondered when he would try to connect one-to-one with me.

"Fine, sir," I said matter-of-factly. "No hostiles."

"Very good," he responded with a somewhat pained look on his face as he turned back. My gaze followed his and I watched as Splint huddled in the corner with three or four other soldiers who were grimly playing cards.

"There are lots of words being thrown around here and some said a little too close to my own name, Atoll. Bureaucrat, pawn, negligent." Bridger looked at me squarely, though he stood at least a head taller. He sighed and looked away, adding in resignation, "I am here to get as many of you home as I can; that's it. Internalize that, Atoll." He inspected my therm with a tilt, nodded once, then walked away.

I turned back to the window and listened to the cacophony of war.

"You hear that?" Tuna asked behind me. He was looking nervously around the bunkhouse, and his eyes went up to the ceiling.

"No... just the normal sounds. Therm fire? Rockets?" I turned quizzically. I was unused to seeing Tuna look so scared; normally, he maintained an expression of neutrality or even good humor during operations. Now, his eyes were circled with darkness and he watched the ceiling frantically.

"I hear it too," Bridger said after a second. I felt silly—this was important and I was missing out. I strained to listen, trying to pick up anything that may have been escaping my notice. Finally, I could hear it. Footsteps. On the roof of the bunkhouse.

"Everyone, to the second floor!" Bridger roared.

Splint and his men leapt to their feet along with the rest of us, and we barged up the narrow steps to the second floor of the building. Hearing the shout, I arrived up the steps just in time to see an Insurrectionist jump through the hole in the ceiling and hit the tiled floor with a thud. He was wearing a red bandana and headband, and wielded an oversized therm rifle with a blade fixed on the end.

A couple of our Sardourian troops were waiting for him, but our comrades weren't experienced with this kind of close-quarters assault. With a single thrust, the Kabat Vi impaled and instantly killed a Sardourian soldier, whose therm rifle was sent careening into the wall. The Insurrectionist wrenched the blade from the limp torso and charged another nearby soldier. That soldier pulled his trigger but the round only left a black and orange cinder circle smoldering in the wall. The Kabat Vi with the bayonet knocked the rifle from his hands and lunged as more enemies lurched through the opening. Just as he lunged, a fresh therm round smashed into the Insurrectionist's skull and brought him down instantly. I caught a glimpse of Orange looking triumphantly smug, but the victory was short-lived. Three more Insurrectionists had jumped through the hole.

They turned to Orange, who stood alone and defiant on a roof's edge on the outer face of a second-story windowsill with her sniper rifle. My heart sank as they raised their therms at her. As I watched, she dropped her sniper rifle seconds before they fired a hail of rounds and she vaulted off the windowsill. I had no idea how she had landed, but it was better than her being shot full of holes by the Kabat Vi. I raised my rifle and fired at them alongside Bridger and Splint, exchanging rounds until all three were dead with only a series of impact marks and splashes of dark blood on the walls from the deadly therm rounds. Splint groaned as he checked the corpses of the two dead Sardourians while the rest of us rushed to the window and looked down. Orange had hit the pavement awkwardly and had probably sustained serious injuries, but she was still alive and trying to drag herself to the door.

Bridger ordered me and another soldier, Herb, to recover Orange. We rushed down the steps and out the door. We threw the door open to find Orange struggling to her feet and attempting to reach for the door. She had already abandoned the burden of her pack and welcomed our support to bring her inside.

"Splint! Get down here! We need a medic!" called Herb. We brought her over to a table in one of the bunkrooms on the first floor and laid her down. We anticipated some kind of surgery would be needed here and Splint was the man for the job… But there was no response from upstairs.

"Splint! We need you!" shouted Herb who grumbled as he opened the door and headed out into the hallway to take the stairs back up. I followed. My nerves were frayed after the consistent hammering we faced by the Insurrection. As we approached the steps, we heard muffled conversation from upstairs. It was hard to make out. We marched up the stairs but stopped suddenly.

The squad had been divided into two subgroups, arrayed across the second floor where fresh corpses still lay. Splint, Tuna, and a few others had just drawn their guns on the rest of the squad. Bridger and Jan reciprocated with rifles raised, and Splint's group seemed prepared to fire at a moment's notice. Many guns turned towards me and Herb as we reached the top of the stairs.

"Get back down there, Atoll!" roared Splint as he pointed a therm at my face. "Clear the door. We're leaving!"

"Treason!" screamed Bridger. A look of cold contempt crossed his face. Jan stood next to him, his augmented eyes mirrored the corporal's disdain. Both had their therms poised for immediate contact, and a look of hardened betrayal emanated from their body language

Splint, for his part, had a wild look of rebellion painted on every feature of his narrowed, angry gaze. Tuna, meanwhile, looked resigned and despondent but nonetheless practiced with his weapon.

"Go ahead. Shoot us then, if we're traitors!" Splint retorted.

Bridger raised his rifle a little higher, but after another tense moment, he couldn't bring himself to do it. "I said, back down the stairs!"

raged Splint, rifle pointed back towards me, spittle flying. I was utterly bewildered, and clearly Herb was too. They were defecting? But why? We needed a medic for Orange!

"Splint, please, we have a serious wound down here..." Herb pleaded.

"Shut up!" Splint bellowed, "Don't say another word."

Bridger opened his mouth, but Splint cut him off.

"I'm done with this outfit, and so are Tuna, Waters, and LaReye. We're done fighting this war, especially in a trash heap of a city for some bureaucrats we'll never meet. Greene was ten times better than you'll ever be, Bridger," he said, spitting.

Waters and LaReye were long-standing career soldiers. This party of escapists had serious backing. This was ridiculous to me. Like the Kabat Vi, we're going to do more poorly disjointed! Splint and his defectors forced us back down the steps and into the hallway before they piled out of the bunkhouse, swearing and shouting as they left. I watched quietly as Splint led the small group far into the parking lot and then out of sight. Once they had cleared the bunkhouse, Bridger solemnly ordered us to take up our defense positions. What remained of our squad took to the windows, rifles raised. The ten of us that remained—half our original force—were silent in taking our positions.

"Not you, Atoll and Herb. I need a report on Orange."

"Her legs took most of the beating from the fall, sir. It was eighteen feet. She's having a real hard time walking... I think something's broken," Herb analyzed. He wasn't a medic, but he'd summed it well.

"Jan, you've got some medic experience, don't you?" Bridger said, turning.

"Yes sir, I do," the augment replied, the implants over his eye flashing. "If it's just a broken bone, I could make a splint—" I winced slightly. He continued, "Or a brace of some kind. The word had clearly impacted Bridger too. He mumbled a bit, nodding and losing his grip on his therm.

"Well... just do that then," he instructed. Jan nodded, saluted, and spun around to enter the room where we had set down the wounded Orange. "How's the perimeter?" he shouted to one of the guards at a window. The guard gave a halfhearted nod to the Corporal, indicating no immediate threat.

The betrayal was shocking, but Splint leaving Orange there to suffer without treatment was worse. The cruelty shocked me. We stayed in the bunkhouse a little while longer while Jan worked to treat Orange. During this time, Bridger tried to shore up our resolve.

"Remember men, we can end this battle. We can save so many lives. Our goal here is simply to take command of downtown. Once we do that, we're done." I was concerned by the tone in his voice—he was trying to be reassuring, to not sound weak. We had already lost nine men, to battle and to defection. While it pained me to lump the heroes who died in the service of Sardouria with the escapees under Splint, the fact remained that, together, they represented almost half of our unit. With the losses, and Orange with no hope of a quick recovery, could we even be sure we'd be able to capture downtown if we made it there, regardless of whatever superior strategic position awaited us?

Hours dragged on with nothing to break up the monotony but the changing of the guard and the sound of larger bombardments. If Splint was still here, he surely would have had something to help

Orange be more comfortable or mobilize sooner. We occupied ourselves with trying to scrub all the blood off the second floor with what limited cleaning supplies were available. It was almost surreal, trying to clean off the blood in a city so mired in it. It seemed unnatural to try and fight the cycle of death that Iron Spires perpetuated. As for the bodies, we covered them with sleeping bags in silence. Tuna had taken the body bags. That is, if there had even been any left.

After almost three hours had passed, Jan emerged from the bunk room, supporting a limping Orange who was wearing a makeshift leg brace. Jan explained that he had to reposition the hip bone. I wondered, do all augments have minor surgery training? I'd have to ask. Orange had been given some anesthetic chemical, but not much, and it was clear she needed more time to recover.

"Thank you, Jan. You performed well." Bridger commended. His eyes, however, showed little pleasure. Instead, they glowered with the dark coldness of shame.

By this point, the bunkhouse was feeling claustrophobic, cursed even. I started to loathe staring at the same walls. With every passing minute, Splint was getting further away and we were stuck in here, twiddling our thumbs and cleaning our weapons. We gave Orange another hour to recover from the procedures, but we were losing valuable time. As Bridger said, the window to seize command of downtown and end this wretched battle could close at any moment, rendering all our suffering fruitless.

The hour ended, and it was time to move out once again. Orange was able to walk at a reduced pace. Under ordinary circumstances, we would likely have called for her to be picked up by aircraft. Bridger picked up his radio to attempt to contact Sardourian Command but set it back down after a moment.

He explained wearily, "'They've got little jamming nests all around the city. We won't be getting anything through to Command." This meant that Orange would have to stick with the group despite her wounds. We solemnly picked up our dwindling gear without comment and filed out of the bunkhouse one by one. Orange was towards the middle now with her sniper rifle slung over her back. With the loss of Splint, Bridger had also been entrusting me with more duties—mundane ones, to be sure, but I felt it was an important development. For instance, I was put in charge of minesweeping and checking for other traps towards the front of the line with Bridger himself. I kept the magnetic device given to me by Tuna, and used it to great effect, uncovering many broom mines underneath roads and sidewalks.

Of course, the scenes of destruction were unparalleled as we made our way into the heart of the city. Crashed aircraft and wrecked vehicles lay everywhere, charred and abandoned hulks shadowed by glassless skyscrapers, blood-soaked sandbags, and veritable mountains of debris and rubble. I even saw the occasional human bone, having spent so long rotting in the untouched corners of the streets since the war opened. Areas like these could not even be considered a warzone, but rather what was left of one. The fighting had so consumed the battleground that barely anything was left unscathed.

Despite all this, occasional points of beauty still shone through the carnage. Just an hour after leaving the bunkhouse, I paused briefly to observe a white tulip sprouting out of a hole in a cracked flak helmet lying on the sidewalk. It was ringed by the cold bodies of many Kabat Vi fighters whose weapons were haphazardly scattered around the street. Clearly, we were entering an even more dangerous sector of the city. It was these inexplicable moments, wherein the persistence of nature was demonstrated to me, that kept me trudging through this phase, the beating heart of the battle. We hid underneath storefront covers, in shadows, and sprinted from cover to cover with a limping Orange in tow. It would have been utterly disastrous to remain exposed for any period of time, but we needed every available trigger finger and could not afford to leave any behind.

We neared downtown, the great pre-war industrial center of Iron Spires and now the bloodiest front of the urban battle for control. Lusiran and Sardourian forces waged their own skirmishes every day against Insurrectionists here in a perpetual, bullet-laden cross between chess and cat-and-mouse.

As we approached, an Insurrectionist appearing in a window or storefront doorway quickly became a regular occurrence. We learned to keep our guard up and dispose of them as quickly as possible with overwhelming fire. A wave of thermal gunfire was enough for most enemies to duck back into their hidey-holes, or, if we got lucky, we'd hit them and end their personal insurrection. We only made the winding trip downtown due to Jan's memorized directions; Waters, who had defected with Splint, was supposed to have been our navigator. With nine soldiers defected or dead, each of us remaining took on additional responsibilities. While this route may not have been the most efficient, we could tell we were on the right path by the growing sounds of therm fire. Through a combination of stealth and luck, we managed to evade most of the Insurrectionists on our journey. It also seemed that the majority of combatants were duking it out in downtown proper. I couldn't imagine being involved in that fighting. As we began to reach a sharp right turn in the street, lined by massive skyscrapers that marked our presence in the wealthier areas of town, Jan ordered us to halt.

"Do not look around that corner!" he shouted. None of us did, pausing before we could turn right. Jan appeared lost in thought, struggling to recall something.

"What is it, Jan? What's around the corner?" Bridger demanded. Jan's implants flashed uncontrollably for a few seconds. I was worried he had short-circuited or something. After a few seconds, his expression cleared.

"The Harmony Plaza," he said, "It's only twelve blocks from downtown, and it's sure to be full of hostiles. Perhaps high-powered vehicles."

"The Insurrectionists have tanks?" I cried with a conclusory jump.

"Only a few," Jan reassured me. "Reserved for strategic locations like this one. The point is, if I had to guess, its therm is all out of ammo. This whole area has been choked by Sardourian interceptor patrols for weeks now. They haven't been able to resupply ammunition to anyone in the Plaza so the tank should only be able to fire with its main cannon."

"That's a big assumption, Jan..." Bridger said, "What are you getting at?"

"A tank easily poses the greatest threat to our squad," the augment continued, "But, if there's one there, we can spread its field of fire by splitting up into two groups and flanking the defenders. With an aggressive push, we can close the distance by charging around the sides of the Plaza, then promptly disabling the vehicle with hand grenades." The rest of us idled awkwardly as Bridger considered the suggestion.

After a moment, he reloaded his therm and decided, "This is why I asked for you, Jan. Load up, everybody!" The Special Operators—what remained of us—rearmed ourselves, adjusted our helmets, and stood at attention. "All right!" Bridger shouted. "I'll be taking one group. Jan will lead the other." He began to rattle off names, dividing us equally between the two strike forces.

"Orange will stay back here to provide fire support with her sniper rifle," he said flatly and quickly. I had mostly stopped listening after being assigned to my group. I was with Bridger's team and would be flanking along the right edge of the Plaza. Each of us had two hand grenades, and the team leaders had four. It was a sizable wealth of them—more than enough to disable a standard battle tank.

The plan was indeed a gamble with a high risk and high reward. To myself, I considered the possibility that Corporal Bridger accepted it out of inward spite for Splint, who had repeatedly criticized Bridger's tactics for being too static. Well, this was the exact opposite of static; a risky, aggressive plan that would take the battle to the Kabat Vi, and on which our mission's fate would hinge.

"On my mark." Bridger ordered. He gestured for me, Herb, and the other few soldiers of his team to group up with him. Jan's group formed up similarly.

"Three..." I tightened my grip on my therm rifle.

"Two..." I clenched my teeth.

"One..."

I thought of home.

"Forward!" bellowed Bridger, as we rushed around the corner in our two groups. I followed close behind the Corporal, hugging the right side of the road. Jan's suspicions were indeed confirmed. A short jog down the road opened up right into the sizable Harmony Plaza which was teeming with several dozen Insurrectionists. However, the main attraction was the big, bulky steel tank parked at the center of the Plaza, at the base of a massive pedestal where a statue of the Lusiran Monarch had been torn down. I saw the Kabat Vi tank crew resting on the armor plate and realized we had taken them by surprise. This was good. We scampered along the side street, Orange covering our assault from behind. As I watched, an Insurrectionist tank crewman was blown apart by one of our therm rounds.

We reached the Plaza, and I followed Bridger, immediately taking off down the right side of the tiled area. Intimidating rows of condominiums lined the whole area, and the tiled ground made for an even more artificial battlefield than I had grown to expect in Iron Spires. I could see the small shapes of the tank crewmen load into the vehicle and close the hatches behind themselves. It would only be a matter of seconds now before they were combat-ready. If the tank's therm still had ammunition, it would shred us quickly. Our whole plan hinged on the tank being reliant on its inaccurate main gun. As we hurried along the right edge of the Plaza, we began to take fire from Kabat Vi infantry. We slowed our pace ever so slightly to give counterfire. I wasn't sure how many we were bringing down at this distance, but they had practically no cover and were easier to target as a result.

On the left side, Jan and his men were rocketing along the side of the Plaza and drawing their fire more intensely. I watched as one of

Jan's men was nailed several times with therm rounds and collapsed onto the tiles with critical wounds. His team still put up a fierce fight.

By that point, the tank had started to rotate on its chassis, stopping only when the main barrel faced us. As we sprinted, I figured that the tank's automatic therm must be out of ammunition, or it would have fired by now. Instead, it fired off the heavy main gun with a terrible boom, sending smoke pouring out and up into the already clouded sky. The shell flew overhead with a whoosh, annihilating a section of condo behind us. I heard no calls for medics from our task force. We continued to hug the right edge as we closed the distance with the tank. A second and third shell went in our direction, both hitting the condo behind us. I shot my rifle from the hip and tried to take out some of the infantry who were defending the vehicle. I forced them to drop to the ground as my barrage impacted harmlessly against the armor of the tank. The tank's metal seemed to radiate with the heat of repeated therm rounds.

Meanwhile, Jan's group was taking heavy fire as they approached the central plaza. They were forced to take cover in large, ornate shrubbery. Despite the continued barrage from the plant cover, most of the defenders shifted their attention to Bridger's team. My team.

Therm fire and tank rounds whipped past us. We were so close. As we closed with the tank and I continued to hip-fire with my rifle at the last of the Insurrectionist infantry, I felt my knee give out followed by a burst of exquisite pain and heat. I had been shot. I rolled in agony as the rest of my team ran by; they couldn't afford to stop running. So far, the tank had been totally unable to hit any moving targets, but as I shifted to look at it, I was met with a bone-chilling sight: it was swiveling to focus on already downed targets. Me.

I watched in terror as the chassis, supporting the huge barrel, rotated. My team was almost there, they could make it. They had to make it.

The main gun was almost pointed at me now. I was vaguely aware of Jan's men launching a desperate charge out of the bushes, and Bridger loosing a grenade at the tank. Two explosions in quick succession rocked the Plaza, sending a shockwave rippling through the area. I braced to be utterly vaporized.

Instead, the smoke rose, and footsteps cut through my anticipation. Through blurry pain, I saw the two squads convene at the burning tank with Orange limping in a moment later. The joint team hurried to check the area for any enemy survivors, but none were found. With help, Orange created a sniper post on the cooling tank carcass. I watched the Sardourian forces fan out around the Plaza, a skeleton crew spread thin. Someone discovered a hidden cache of therm rounds which Herb quickly distributed. When he got to me, he helped me to my feet and pulled a tube from his pack.

"Uh. Here. It will... soothe the burn," he relayed. His words were marked with anxious separation. I gingerly uncapped the tube and squeezed the gelatinous blue chemical onto my cindered knee. It stung mightily but faded with a sparking and tingling sensation. Finally, a refreshing coolness subsumed the entire face of my knee. I felt my hair follicles rise with the sensation.

Bridger shouted orders before forming up with Jan, Herb, and a heavily augmented soldier who I'd never talked to before. "We're within striking range now, sir," Jan informed the Corpora. "But we absolutely must wait until we are at full strength before attempting to seize control of the downtown area." I approached the squadron.

A sudden ringing in my ears didn't help, and I braced myself against a small potted tree resting nearby.

"...disappeared during the fighting. I'll record him as MIA," I heard Jan finish.

I asked, with a bit of a slur to my words, "Who disappeared?"

"Roach, a Private. He was a Construction Legion graduate in Jan's team. It's why they were so hard-pressed to counter the Insurrection's fire; they had lost their machine gunner," Bridger explained. Jan nodded gravely.

"Well, what do you think happened?" I asked. "The tank was hardly shooting at your team, so it's not like it could've..." I hesitated, "pulverized him or something." The four men nodded assent.

"We think he went off to defect," the heavily augmented man said. He had more than three times as many implants as Jan. They lined his arms and were positioned all across his head and face. He had mechanical augments in his shoulders and wrists, and implants over both eyes. He kept his face obscured by a black bandana.

"Splint and his gang doubled back. They're tailing you," he continued. "Have been since just after you left the bunkhouse. They want your—or I should say our—guns and equipment." He stepped forward to shake my hand. "Specialist Razor. I was Greene's spotter during the counter-guerrilla campaign. Now, I've been scouting Iron Spires for the Corporal and Jan here," he explained.

"Private Atoll, Construction Legion," I replied.

"It's a good thing you met us here, Razor. You can see, we need every able trigger we can find." Bridger turned to me and it seemed a tired pride had replaced his earlier shame. "Atoll, we're hard-pressed to hold this Plaza for any period of time. In fact, we're going to abandon it as soon as the other wounded wake up and can walk. Downtown is our priority, not this place."

I nodded in understanding.

"Anything you can do to help our guards over at the downtown-facing road, it'd be much appreciated," Bridger said.

Wait. He's referring to my skills as an engineer!

"Understood, sir," I responded with an energized salute. Herb saluted as well and gestured for me to follow him. He was clearly an infantry man through and through, with a medal on his chest to indicate Great Service in the war against the Kabat Vi. I slightly struggled to keep my balance as we walked to the far edge of the Plaza where two of our men stood with raised rifles pointed down the street, ready for whatever came next.

"We need more cover," I surmised instantly. That was the start of my great engineering project. I pried metal debris from everywhere and hurriedly welded together crude metal walls and barricades with flat bottoms so they wouldn't fall over. The grunts thanked me and quickly set them up. I turned back and saw the other two wounded were helped to their feet. We wouldn't be getting much use out of my barricades, but at least they had provided me with something to do.

Bridger raised his arm to call everyone to him and then walked over to my position at the barricades. He shook my hand briefly for my work before turning to address the entire squad.

"We're on the cusp of a great, great victory," he addressed them all. "Only twelve blocks down that road," he pointed, "is our strategic destination which we will exploit to take command of the entire area. We will face the most intense Insurrection resistance we've ever seen, and not all of us may make it back. But I will do everything in my power to make sure that you do get back home to Sardouria and we end this damn war!" he shouted.

"Yes, sir!" we replied.

Many of us were now bandaged, but it wouldn't stop us from getting the job done. We loaded our therms once again, and Bridger called us to form a line. He was going to do this the formal way. He made his way to the front of the line and strode his way down.

"Private Adir!" he shouted to the man in front of me.

"Battle-ready!" Adir responded.

Bridger continued. "Private Atoll!" he shouted. I shifted my grip on my therm.

"Battle-ready!"

He went on. "Private First Class Herb!" "Private Howie!" "Specialist J4... Jan!" Each call out was met with a stalwart cry of "Battle-ready!"

The line was remarkably short, shorter than any unit I'd ever been in that had gone into battle the formal way. He had already neared the end.

"Specialist Razor!" he called, as a strange whine grew in the distance.

"Battle-ready!" came the response from the augmented trooper.

"Private Santan!" Bridger shouted. The call of "Battle-ready!" was drowned out as several aircraft raced overhead. Low-altitude bombers... They must be mounting their final push on downtown. Could we be beating the Insurrection?

Several more aircraft raced overhead. At such extreme speed, I struggled to identify from what country they originated. I shifted my focus and began to listen intently to the sound of the engines. After a few seconds, I identified them as Sardourian models. As they flew, they released whistling payloads into the street between the Plaza and downtown. I watched in apprehension as the devices plummeted down.

"They're lighting the way!" screamed Bridger, "Let's go!"

We rushed into the street towards downtown as quickly as we could and accommodated the soldiers whose injuries required slower movement. Everyone was silent, unsure of what we were witnessing, until the clusters hit the pavement and detonated violently.

"Steam bombs!" yelled Bridger, "Cover your faces!"

Massive and billowing gas plumes poured over themselves towards the Plaza.

"Get your cloths outs!" Jan shouted as he whipped a cloth from his pack and covered his face. The rest of us followed suit just as the gas began to hit us. I grabbed my own cloth in the nick of time, pressing it against my face and holding it there. The gas crashed into us with horrifying speed, ushering in a wave of excruciation like no other. All my exposed skin felt like it was boiling. My neck and hands burned acutely, and it felt as though the gas was eating away at my flesh. Several soldiers began to scream. I, myself, came very close to joining their screams as I internally pleaded for it to stop. The heat didn't heed my pleas. It was relentless and torturous. I knew not to let it into my eyes or mouth, so I kept the cloth tightly pressed against my face. I dared not speak or even cough for fear it might blow the cloth and expose my face to the gas. A few obstinate tears escaped my eyes into the cloth.

After several minutes, relief came. The wind slowly dispersed the gas from the steam bombs until Jan finally declared it safe to withdraw the cloth. My hands, neck, and ankles were stinging and scalded, but above all I craved the fresh air. Our squad was a pretty pathetic sight then, mostly on our knees and grabbing our canteens, splashing water all over the exposed areas. For a little while, no one tried talking to each other; the relief from the horrible gas was enough to render one speechless. Herb's cooling cream quickly ran out as I shared it with anyone with an outstretched palm. Jan studied the more intense chemical burns and applied what he could to treat them. I hated to admit that Splint was the better medic. Bridger struggled to regain control of the situation. Everyone was recovering from an agonizing experience, but now there was also an element of anger. Why did our own planes drop steam bombs so close to active Sardourian troops?

The simple answer was that they had no way of knowing that Bridger's Special Operators were the ones in charge of the Plaza. However, that would not very easily satisfy the battered, fatigued, and burned troops of the Special Operators.

"Try to cool yourselves off, we have to move," Bridger said grimly. The mood had taken a beating.

"Yes, sir," came the chorus of tired soldiers.

I poured water on the cloth and dabbed my neck. Others were stowing their cloths and drawing their weapons once again. I didn't want to seem weak, so I quickly stoppered my own bottle and put away my cloth. My skin still stung, but at least it wasn't torturous pain like I had experienced in the thick of the gas. Bridger ran to the front of the squad.

"Let's try this again," he said, stoic and weary. We drew our therms and continued the twelve-block journey to downtown. This area had been hit hard by the steam bombs—I saw bloated and burnt Insurrectionist corpses hanging out of windows all along the journey. Only a few seemed to have survived. When they revealed themselves, we sent a hail of rounds their way. I wasn't worried about broom mines in this area. The streets were already ripped up, so I predicted any mines that had previously been here were already detonated. With each block we passed, the sounds of fighting downtown grew. Soon, the familiar whine of aircraft returned. Everyone recognized it now, taking out our cloths and stowing our rifles. However, the planes dropped their payloads somewhere downtown. I watched the billowing cloud of gas waft over the high-rises of downtown.

"We're pounding it!" Herb shouted as we drew our weapons once again.

The sounds of eternal conflict were now ominously close. It was getting late. Now, afternoon was turning to evening and the skies had darkened as we reached the end of the street. We had faced eerily limited resistance. As we tightened up our charge formation, Bridger gave us a significant look. It was one I hadn't seen on his face before; if I had to hazard a guess, it was one of pride.

We sprinted out onto the boulevard, therms raised, and witnessed the true scale of the fighting downtown. This was the widest street in the city, which held eight rows of traffic, but I could barely recognize it as such. It was ripped up, bombed out, and nearly entirely coated in rubble and debris. Destroyed vehicles from some long-ago blast were arrayed in a semicircle about two blocks down. From our position, we could see dozens, maybe hundreds, of men fighting from rooftops, windowsills, doorways, barricades, and encampments. Rockets and therm fire went everywhere, and the sound of men screaming permeated everything.

It looked like the Insurrectionists were putting up a good fight despite the recent steam bombing, counterattacking and resisting the Sardourians every step of the way. However, the aftershocks of the bombing were still clearly visible. I could see several bloated and charred corpses strewn about. As we came out onto the boulevard, I took note of an enormous structure that appeared to be made of steel and some kind of reinforced glass. Huge wrought-iron letters adorning the face of the building read "AUG-TEK."

III

"THERE! THAT'S OUR STRATEGIC DESTINATION!" Bridger shouted. The Aug-Tek building was obviously well-guarded by a patrol of Kabat Vi, but we were not going to let that stop us. We drew our weapons and made our way from cover to cover until we were within a hundred feet of the guards. I could see that, at one point, the Aug-Tek building could be accessed by a set of sleek rotating doors, but these had been blown up. The metal pieces were strewn all around, leaving only a void in the front wall. Presently, we were sheltered behind a shattered combat car, reloading our guns before we stormed the place.

"Are you ready, Special Operators?" Bridger barked under his breath. We all nodded; even the wounded seemed ready. "On my mark... three... two..." I quickly surveyed the downtown area to be sure we weren't about to get flanked or sniped down. Seemed clear. Then I felt silly for thinking that Jan wouldn't have already checked. "One... Mark!"

We stood low, leveled our rifles, and streamed like water around a great boulder to attack the bewildered group of Insurrectionists at the doors. They raised their therms to fight back, but we fell upon them with vicious determination, our rounds striking all but one. The remaining Insurrectionist raised his hands in surrender, dropping his therm.

"We can't deal with a prisoner right now!" shouted Bridger.

"We can't let him run off either," Jan replied.

"What if we bind him here?" Orange suggested.

"I don't see why we can't just take him along as a POW," Herb put in.

A terse debate broke out, which drew our attention from the prisoner himself to Bridger and the others. I didn't notice until the last second that the man had drawn a hand grenade and was lobbing it toward us.

"Scatter!" I shouted with the full force that my voice could muster. Trained to do just that on command, Bridger, Jan, and Herb leapt away, while Orange could only limp away before it detonated. Shrapnel went everywhere, but most of it embedded in the pavement. However, several pieces had lodged in the back of Orange's flak armor. Thankfully, nothing had struck an unarmored area. The Insurrectionist, meanwhile, rose and drew a thick blade to the nearest Sardourian, Razor.

Razor was prepared; his augments made him more than a match for the Kabat Vi. He deftly drew a machete from his belt and clashed blades with the Insurrectionist, keeping himself well-guarded. It was clear that, while the Kabat Vi had the advantage of brute strength, Razor was far more skilled. Wielding such a heavy weapon, the Insurrectionist struggled to parry Razor's intense offensive drive with the machete. Razor deftly plunged the sharp edge of his machete deep into the Insurrectionist's clavicle, then withdrew it and pirouetted his momentum to lodge the blade sideways into the left bicep, and finally landed a crossway blow to the Insurrectionist's jugular which left a nearly detached head on a body which tumbled prone. The heavier blade hit the pavement with a metallic thud next to the limp, dirty, lifeless body. Razor confiscated it with a look of victory in his eyes. The victory was short-lived.

"Inside, now!" Bridger ordered. We hurried through the cavity in the wall and into the Aug-Tek building.

It was a scene of great splendor. The front lobby of the building was vast and lined with desks, couches, and other furniture. Aug-Tek had surely been a wealthy company. Now, its headquarters would be our base of operations to seize control of the downtown area. Our goal was within reach, and I was getting ahead of myself. We swept the entire lobby, looking for anything out of the ordinary.

With the Special Operators spreading out to cover more ground, we secured the whole area in short order.

"No hostiles!" called Jan, a shout which was echoed by Orange, Herb, Razor, and the others. Bridger nodded, satisfied.

"We'll have to secure the whole building," he ordered.

I could imagine all manner of traps and threats the Kabat Vi would have rigged up to stop us throughout the tall building.

We'd come this far, and certainly weren't going to take any half measures. The entire Aug-Tek building would need to be secured in order to take command of the downtown area. Two sets of stairs led up to elevators, so we split up into our old teams from the Plaza attack. It was clear that Aug-Tek didn't believe in emergency staircases, with the elevators being the only visible way to travel between floors. There would be no cover in an elevator if enemies were on the other side, but that was an unfortunate risk we had to take for the sake of our mission. I now believed wholeheartedly in this operation. This battle—this suffering—it had to end. The Kabat Vi would be brought to justice. This one building stood in our way of doing so, and I was determined to pacify it.

I followed Bridger up the stairs to the elevator on the right, joined by Herb and a few others. Orange couldn't stay down on the first floor alone, so she joined Jan's group. She had stowed her sniper rifle and was using a standard therm.

Both groups queued the elevator at the same time, and Bridger called, "Just go to the second floor!" We were going to take this one level at a time.

So we did. We waited tensely in the elevator as it squealed up to the second floor. When the doors opened, we were treated to a long hallway lined with office doors. This was clearly an administrative level. Jan's group came out at the same time as ours. Most of the lightbulbs were broken, and the few that flickered provided pitiful light. We were forced to draw electric torches and darklenses to see. Then, we began a simple procedure: kick open an office door, hurriedly check it for hostiles, and get out. It was using this process that we combed through the entire floor in a matter of minutes, no Kabat Vi to be found.

"How many floors are there?" Herb asked Bridger.

"Sixty, I think," Bridger replied. My heart sank. We'd be here all night, with only the sounds of the nearby battle to keep us company.

"I think we'll try to do this a quicker way," Bridger said to the squad once we had cleared the whole hallway and reassembled at the elevators. "My team will go up to the third floor, Jan's will take the fourth, I'll take fifth, and we'll alternate from there. If you find any hostiles, just shout real loud or shoot. The other team will come running."

Jan nodded and saluted, taking his team into an elevator. While he seemed fine with the assignment, I noticed he'd worn a strange look on his face ever since we'd entered the building. It was a haunted expression, as if he were recalling a painful memory. Perhaps there was nothing to it, but I thought otherwise. Jan didn't usually show expressions, not even in the heat of combat or at the betrayal of a defection.

I made one last mental note of the hallway before stepping into the elevator with my team, and we headed up to the third floor. Over the course of the next several hours, we made our way from floor to floor, all hallways and the occasional laboratory or storage room to break up the monotony. There were no Insurrectionists anywhere to be found—our greatest danger came from tripwires set up years ago and the horrific smell. Aug-Tek absolutely reeked, and I had no idea why. It reminded me of the pungent rot of fermenting fruit languishing beneath the outstretched limbs of vibrant fruit trees back home.

It was the dead of night now; I could tell by the slight reduction in violence outside. *What if Insurrectionists take refuge here for the night? We just finished clearing dozens of floors...* I thought wearily. The repetition was seriously wearing on me, but I didn't let it show. I tried to hold my therm in a combat-ready position, but I had lost much of my resolve. Honestly, at this point, it was more surprising that we had not seen any Insurrectionists yet after covering almost sixty floors.

We arrived at the 59th level, which served as a kind of company archive for Aug-Tek. Huge file cabinets and bookshelves lined the room, containing what was surely a plethora of valuable, juicy secrets about the pre-war corporation. One thing was strange, though: the use of paper records. Definitely an outmoded practice. Inspecting the room, I realized it would be harder for governments or outside observers to track paper records. Bridger completely skipped past the massive file cabinets. We fanned out—my darklens had long since died, so I was relying on the beam of light from my electric torch. The archives were easily the smallest level of the building, and we quickly deduced that it was empty. I took a moment to study some nearby shelves and saw an old, slightly tattered book with "TOP SECRET" lettered on its binding. Overcome with curiosity, I reached for the book and cracked it open.

To my disappointment, the book only contained boring, years-old income history and tax information. Meanwhile, Bridger focused on dismantling a large tripwire. Dropping the book, I inspected more of the room's contents but found only dozens of years' worth of company statistics that were meaningless to me. I was becoming so adjusted to it that the sight of a long-dead Lusiran trooper caused me to give a loud start. Bridger turned and ran over to me, spotting the man almost instantly. The Corporal leaned in to inspect the man's uniform and identifying patches.

"This man wasn't a combat soldier," he deduced. He was a high-ranking officer. What was he doing poking around in the archives at…the time of the insurrection?" Indeed, the body was heavily decomposed—little more than a skeleton—and had likely been lying in that same position since the uprising had brought the city under the control of the Kabat Vi years earlier.

We carefully searched him for identification, finding no weapons in the process. He must have submitted to a search by Aug-Tek security before entering, unusual during the period of military tension that preceded the insurrection. Ultimately, we found a rectangular card in one of his pockets that identified him as Lieutenant General Spade, attaché of the Lusiran military command, as well as a negotiator between the government and Aug-Tek. As we pulled out the card, however, a small handheld notebook also slipped out of the same pocket. Worn and visibly aged, I handled it with extreme care. A yellow ribbon acted as a bookmark. Curious, I opened the marked page.

The notebook was scrawled with small lettering that covered every inch of paper. Spade had been taking very detailed notes about the company and its practices, including seemingly mundane details like the number of doors in a hallway. As Bridger studied the pages over my shoulder, my attention was drawn to a circled passage that described a room known as the "originator," but the rest of the page was mostly empty. I pointed the term out to Bridger. For a moment, he seemed lost in thought. His brow furrowed as he took the notebook from me and scrutinized the passage.

He looked confused for another moment before shouting, "TO THE ELEVATOR!"

As we started sprinting towards the elevator, I heard shouts and movement above us. Jan's group had reached level 60 and something was happening. I sprinted into the elevator, adjusted my helmet, and steeled myself for the next floor. We jostled upward for a few seconds and heard the sounds of shouting grow more pronounced. Bridger nodded to each one of us as we checked and raised our therms. The elevator doors opened and we rushed out into a massive, open room. The walls were lined top-to-bottom with rows of strange pods, made almost exclusively of frosted dark glass and accessible by narrow steel walkways and a network of ladders. Each pod was a little bigger than a coffin. What was this place? The far wall did not have any pods. Instead, it was a huge floor-to-ceiling window that overlooked the massive metropolis. Through it, I could see that daylight was beginning to break over Iron Spires.

At the center of the room was a raised platform that was furnished with several large metal control stations and lights. More than a dozen Kabat Vi lay dead, bloody and decaying.

I whipped my head around and, to my horror, discovered Tuna, Splint, and the other defectors hurling vicious insults at Jan and his men. It was another standoff. Jan wore the same look on his face I had seen earlier: a mixture of regret and apprehension. Now, it was compounded by a true rage. He, Orange, and Razor all brandished therms. Jan was not taking the bait, instead allowing Splint to shout obscenities while his gang tried to sabotage the control stations. The defectors looked much worse for wear—they had clearly experienced several scrapes with the Kabat Vi—but something didn't add up. How were they able to get up here before us?

As if to answer my unspoken question, Jan turned to face Bridger as we joined his group, weapons raised at Splint.

"They sidestepped the Plaza and came here following an alternate route. Must've come through a back entrance. I'm surprised they're still alive," he said with disgust.

My eyes fell on a Sardourian corpse lying on the ground near one of the control panels. I squinted until I recognized the face. It was Roach, the fellow Construction Legion graduate, the one who had abandoned Jan's team at the Plaza. His body looked decayed longer than was possible and flies circled his putrid, lifeless form.

I swallowed my disgust at the defectors and turned. "Roach must've gone after Splint!" I shouted to Bridger. He nodded hurriedly, but it clearly was not the foremost topic on his mind. His jaw was set in a hard line as he faced Splint.

The defector looked deranged, holding his therm loosely and irresponsibly. His other goons, Waters and LaReye, looked no better.

"Stay back, spineless Sards!" Waters shouted at us with a gleam in his eye that scared me more than Splint. However, he foolishly dual-wielded therm rifles. He'd get almost no accuracy holding them like that. I bit my cheek as I resisted retorting and instead tasted the bile bitterness of revenge on my tongue.

"How about you step back from those panels, Splint?" demanded Bridger with eyes narrowed.

Splint laughed, "Not on your life. You don't give me orders anymore, remember?" he taunted. Bridger responded with a low growl between his teeth.

"What're you doing over at those stations, anyway?" Jan demanded to know. Just then, I noticed Tuna was dismantling pieces of the pods and their metallic mechanisms that seemed to hold the modules together.

"Oh, you don't have any idea, do you, augment? I would've thought you would be more familiar with the process."

Jan looked taken aback, lowering his therm a bit. "No, you don't mean…" Splint threw back his head and guffawed, a mean-spirited laugh that was aimed to wound.

"Yes, of course I do!" he shouted with glee.

Jan spun to face Bridger, saying, "Sir, they're going to release—"

It was too late; Splint and his gang of defectors opened fire. They sprayed our squad with therm rounds, and we charged forward. Our counterattack was accurate and powerful, but they had superior firepower with stronger therms. As we charged, Waters's double rifles sent a wave of rounds everywhere, striking one of our men in the face with a terminal round.

Herb shouted in despair at the sight of our comrade's death.

"Adir!" he cried, dropping to try to revive the crumpled soldier. Herb was horribly exposed. I shot at Waters as I advanced, but my rounds impacted harmlessly against the control station he used as a shield. Everything was going wrong—I heard the click of my empty magazine and replaced it in a sweat-soaked rush.

LaReye, grinning, fired once at Herb who kneeled next to Adir. A single round from Orange blasted through his head and ended LaReye's life. LaReye's round had missed Herb by inches.

"You're too slow!" bellowed Splint as he tapped Tuna, who was still crouched and working on disassembling a control station. A moment later, Tuna jolted suddenly before collapsing to the floor motionless. Distant mechanical sounds punctuated the air. The rattle of gunfire and shouts of the wounded echoed against the walls as the many pods slowly swiveled open.

"You're releasing them before they've been educated!" Jan shouted, trading fire with Splint.

"That's the idea, Jan! They're going to need a bit of practice if they want to bring peace to this city!" responded Splint, his screams dripping with malice. Plumes of an unknown gas billowed from the opening pods as human forms extricated themselves. For a second, I caught a glimpse of the internal mechanisms of the pods; they were like chair mounts, holding the augments in seated positions. I saw automated surgical equipment attached to robotic arms within some of the pods.

"They're augments! Untrained," Jan screamed. "They're feral!" He and Splint continued firing back and forth from cover.

I turned my rifle up towards the hundreds of fresh figures as they lumbered out onto the walkways above us. They paused briefly to observe the scene and our terrified faces below. Suddenly, they pitched themselves over the side rails and impacted with the primary floor, each with a horrifyingly dense thud. They rose slowly with pops of bone and sinew realigning and sprinted directly towards us. This was a nightmare.

The defectors were forced to defend their position from all sides, gunning down any augments that got too close, while we were quickly overrun and forced to give up much of the ground we had gained against Splint's men. The augments were fast, tough, and primal. I expended several magazines keeping them off me; they proved to be superb bullet-eaters. A look of triumph etched across Splint's face as his defectors rebuffed the sprinting augments. Meanwhile, we steadily retreated, falling back as augments reached us and ripped into our fragmented squad. One feral lurched at Private Santan and gnawed a chunk out of him, sending him stumbling to the ground in a fit of agony. Some of them picked up dropped guns and engaged us at range, putting us even more on the defensive. I kept a firm grip on my therm and targeted the ones grabbing at the spare weaponry. There were just so many, and they kept coming. Waters did a remarkable job obliterating them with his dual rifles as he laughed maniacally.

Tuna had pulled himself to his feet and seemed perturbed at the control panel. He shouted something to Splint. I couldn't hear what was said, but it made Splint furious. He raged at Tuna while still firing on the augments. I refocused as an augment advanced on my position. I dropped my therm and drew my machete as it threw a mighty fist towards my head. I sidestepped and cut a deep gash into its arm with my blade. In the same motion, I brought the machete down and hacked into its leg, sending it careening to its knees. I caught Waters shifting his footing towards me before he unleashed a barrage of rounds in my direction. As the blazing thermal bullets tore apart the walls around me, I saw the augment before me slump lifeless. I grabbed its body and used it to shield myself from Waters's onslaught. Thermal rounds pounded into the corpse as I dragged it and myself closer to my protective squad.

The fighting intensified. Jan and Bridger engaged the augments at close range with pistols. Orange stayed near the elevator to snipe the ones who grew too close to our men. Several were struggling in frenzied hand-to-hand combat. I sheathed my machete and withdrew my own pistol, still using the augment corpse to partially shield me from the barrage. I fired across the room into the flank of the roiling mass of augments. There was little need for accuracy; there was no way I could miss.

As the firefight continued, I noticed a growing whine was filling the air, joining the cacophony of therm fire, shouts, and feet (and bodies) hitting the floor. After a moment, Splint noticed as well, and took it as a cue to resume his tirade against Tuna while barraging the lethal augments.

It was a matter of seconds before a gunship came into view outside the shattered windows of this floor. Hovering just outside was a great, gray aircraft supported by four heavy rotors and carrying the largest Sardourian side-guns I had ever seen. Whatever tampering Tuna had been doing to the electrical systems must have alerted Sardourian forces. The gunship hovered into view just outside the huge floor-to-ceiling windows as the dawning sun rose behind it, casting a brilliant orange outline to the hulking ship.

The pilot looked like he was shouting into a headset. The gunship's rotors added just another layer of noise to the growing chaos of the battle. For a moment, I was paralyzed by irrational fear that the ship would try to launch steam bombs. I stopped firing on the main cluster of augments for a moment to gather my bearings.

Waters turned to fire a stream of therm rounds into the gunship, but they merely deflected off its heavy armor. After a moment, an unbroken line of rounds, marked by the loudest buzz of gunfire I had ever heard, emitted from the weapons on the gunship. The remaining glass panels shattered violently and the walls melted away.

The torrent of firepower also obliterated much of the central console that Tuna was fiddling with. Desperately, he attempted to finish connecting wires, punching buttons, and flipping switches. He swiveled and shouted an affirmative to Splint whose face contorted into a soulless grin as he slapped Tuna on the back.

With work apparently complete, the defectors dropped to the ground. Splint shouted something in our direction but was drowned out by the fire from the gunship. The heavy, ship-mounted guns also blasted apart dozens of the augments. I turned to see a giant augment with massive metal fists swinging at Bridger.

The exhausted corporal was outmatched. Undoubtedly, he was seasoned with the machete, but the hulking beast of an augment was absurdly strong, fresh from his pod, and ready to drown battlefields in blood. With the two combatants so close together, it would be far too risky to open fire; I nonetheless raised my pistol in case a clear shot arose.

As the melee continued, my Sardourian comrades advanced to mount a counterattack against the remaining augments. After a misplaced swing by Bridger, the augment grabbed his wrist and painfully wrenched the machete out of his hands. I fired on the augment, but my meek pistol did little more than poke annoying holes in the wild humanoid. No one else had a good angle to take a shot against the augment for fear of hitting Bridger. The machete clattered down.

Razor sprinted in suddenly and tackled the augment. They wrestled furiously. He stood a fighting chance with his own enhanced abilities. He tussled with the creature on the concrete floor. They rolled, punched, and choked—a battle of good augment versus bad, with Razor leveraging everything he could to subdue his opponent in this deadly game.

A crack suddenly perforated the cavernous room as the feral augment broke Razor's neck, released his body, and stood up. Its expression was blank and uncaring. With nothing blocking our shot, we opened fire on it with our pistols. It was down in a matter of moments. Fueled by adrenaline and rage, we surged forward to mop up the last augments with tenacity. Jan ran to Razor's broken corpse while the rest of us moved to capture the control stations. While Jan mourned, it was still business for us as we ripped through the remaining augments methodically.

I tried to ignore the growing emptiness that was building up inside me as I coldly raised my weapon and approached the center pedestal. I was surrounded by dozens of dead or injured soldiers and augments, but I forced myself to keep taking the next steps forward. Out of the corner of my eye, I could see a mass of writhing, limbless augments on the floor.

The defectors remained lying down and out of sight until Tuna jumped up with a therm rifle and shot a burst of fire at us. We raised our own guns which forced him back behind cover. As I watched, more gunships approached the broken windows. Justice was closing in. Splint and Waters leapt to their feet and sprinted back to the windy cavity overlooking the city. We mercilessly opened fire on them as they ran. Waters returned fire but there was no point in the face of our overwhelming firepower. Eventually, he dropped both of his therms.

They stood at the precipice, sixty stories in the air, as we formed a semicircle around them. We advanced.

Bridger kept his gun pointed at Splint's head as he spat, "You still have time to surrender."

Splint barked with laughter. "Please," he said. "It'll be the same fate, just a little delayed." To his right, Waters nodded. Three Sardourian gunships had drawn close, bringing with them a new symphony of engine noises hovering outside the shattered windows.

"You'll get a trial," Bridger promised, to which Splint released another hissing noise—a gross approximation of laughter. We were in the dark final stages of this mission, and I desperately wanted to bring Splint to justice. "I'll ask one more time—" Bridger started, but he was cut off by a shout as Splint drew a pistol and opened fire, shooting wildly. I couldn't tell who he had hit, but to his left, Waters drew a gun of his own.

My vision blurred. I suddenly felt dizzy, and pain was blossoming across my chest... I looked down. Adrenaline bled into excruciation as realization hit me harder than the therm round. Splint shot me! I started to panic, watching in stunned silence as rounds impacted against Waters's chest. He faltered and gripped at his chest as he stumbled over the window's edge. He slipped out of sight without so much as a whisper of noise. Splint's gun jammed and he threw it at Bridger in frustration.

As Bridger rushed to apprehend Splint, the only sound I heard above the roar of gunship engines and clatter of distant gunfire was Jan; he was crying. Finally looking down in shock, I swayed for a moment, then stumbled.

Herb? I couldn't tell who, but someone lowered me onto a stretcher. I hazily realized I was passing through one of the large broken windows by several soldiers. The next moment, I blinked and saw the metallic inside of a gunship, motors rattling its occupants. The cocktail of pain and terror overwhelmed me.

Everything became a blur. I finally succumbed to exhaustion amid a soundtrack of aggressive gunship rotors whirring.

What felt like seconds later, I opened my eyes to see Bridger and Herb looming over me. I rolled my head side to side and realized I had been moved to a cot, stripped of my armor, and heavily bandaged around my torso.

"You got shot three times, Atoll," Herb said. I groaned and tried to see more. Sardourian and Lusiran soldiers who I'd never seen before milled around, talking and planning. Had we done it? Taken control of downtown? There were far fewer sounds of fighting than before. Through the windows, I could see the midday sun beaming down.

Spears of pain lanced through my stomach at three points, just as he said, but the sensation was dulled by what I could only assume was high-quality medicine.

"The impact wounds will heal fairly quickly," the corporal explained, "but the internal damage will take months. You'll have to get more medicine when you return to Sardouria. We only have a small amount." I nodded ever so slightly.

"Sir, what's our status?" I asked weakly. Bridger stared blankly for a moment before allowing a light smile to spread across his face.

"The Aug-Tek building is secure, reinforcements have arrived, and downtown is on the verge of total collapse. All active units stationed at Talon Base are assaulting now. Our infiltration caused major disruption of their forces, and they've lost ground elsewhere. Iron Spires is projected to fall within a couple of weeks."

Relief washed over me, as did the feeling of incalculable accomplishment. Were we the last straw that tipped the scale of the war against the Kabat Vi? Surely not—there were many other Insurrectionist strongholds other than Iron Spires. I refocused on the immediacy of my surroundings. I sat up with Herb's help and saw my equipment piled on the ground nearby.

"Where's Jan?" I inquired.

"Inspecting the squad," Bridger said simply. "We're waiting for the rest of the gunships to touch down so we can haul our entire squad out of here. You're going back to Sardouria, to a remote outpost called Silver Point. It's deep in friendly territory and the only military camp with the medical facilities to effectively treat your wounds. I assumed you'd be brought out of the service after this, but the war effort is still in full swing."

Bridger's words carried a brief tone of bitterness. Or was it resentment? Perhaps Bridger didn't like the newest orders from Command.

Home.

I was going back. To Sardouria. Away from this city of carnage. I had seen more violence than in three campaigns abroad combined. The thought of home reassured me, relaxed me, and then scared me. I felt bitter about Silver Point, the medical facility in my homeland, but for very different reasons than I would have had a month ago. Back then, I would have felt cheated, my engineer's diploma wasted on an assignment that could be written off almost as a vacation. But now, I hesitated because Silver Point still wasn't home. I had seen the darkest side of war. Back at Silver Point, I'd probably be among people who had never even crossed the border into Lusira. They'd see me at my worst: confused, unwelcomed, and foreign. There, I could not possibly conduct myself as clearly as I could to my comrades in the heat of battle.

Corporal Bridger explained, "There are still unanswered questions. Whatever those defectors were trying to do, they did it. The only immediate effects were massive interference on most Sardourian and Lusiran communications channels. Our specialists pinpointed the source and sent a gunship. As far as we know, there weren't any other effects, but there's really no way to know until something else happens."

So the defectors had accomplished one small victory in the end. I grimaced.

"We'll let you rest." Bridger said, motioning for Herb to follow. I looked painfully across the active floor. In the time I was unconscious, the Aug-Tek building had been converted to a stronghold, reinforced with barricades, and converted to a new command center. Supplies, weapons, food, and medicine had been delivered in vast quantities and were being closely guarded. Order appeared well maintained.

I watched as a column of troops escorted Splint outside and an approaching gunship whirred in the distance. I flipped around to find Jan standing nearby. He looked worn.

"Hey, Jan," I said tiredly

Stiffly, Jan responded, "I am inspecting the status of our troops. How are you feeling, Atoll?"

"Never been better," I said with a smile. "But how about you?"

Jan's gaze drifted and he stared off. Turning to look back at me, he answered, "I was educated by Aug-Tek when I was first augmented." In an unexpected and indirect fashion, he added, "Desecrating my birthplace and then witnessing the death of my closest comrade."

"I am sorry about Razor. He died saving the corporal's life. He was a hero," I offered.

He snapped his attention back to me.

"Thank you, Private," he said.

The approaching gunships grew louder, and he turned to leave. I called after him, "Don't regret being an augment, Jan." I imagined his thoughts were crowded with imagery of the ferals that brutally assaulted us, and more specifically, ended the life of his friend.

He spun around to face me and said matter-of-factly, "I do not. It is a critical part of my identity. As was my time in Iron Spires. Thank you, Private Atoll." He spun on his heel and left to report to Bridger. As I watched through the windows of the Aug-Tek lobby, multiple gunships touched down in the street outside. With hands cuffed and head low, Splint was loaded onto one of the ships.

Herb trotted over to me and said, "It's time to go, Atoll."

I grunted... I wasn't sure I was ready to go. The thought of Silver Point still sat ominously atop a pile of disjointed thoughts. I struggled to my feet, and he gingerly helped me to where Bridger and Jan were waiting. The rest of the squad was assembled in alphabetical order, so I joined them. With the death of Adir in the Battle of the 60th floor, I was now at the head of the line.

"We did a good thing these past few days," Bridger said, walking up and down the line. "Some of you will be changed by it, but we ended this battle. The Insurrection in Iron Spires is finished and it's thanks to this squad," he commended with an assertive nod.

I wasn't sure what he was doing when he called out, "Terrence!"

The Private at the other end of the line shouted, "Ready for home!"

Then it registered. He was giving one final formal acknowledgement to his troops before we returned to Sardouria. It was a old tradition that had fallen out of use over the course of the war, when the lengths of service began to increase. I wasn't sure why Bridger was doing it now.

Bridger side-stepped and called, "Santan!"

"Ready for home!"

I was cautious at returning to Sardouria, but I knew, much like Jan, that my time here would be a part of me for years to come. I didn't fear it, though. I had fought as hard as I could to stop a dangerous and oppressive organization. I knew it to be true: Bridger was proud of me.

"Orange!"

"Ready for home!" she shouted, sniper rifle on her back and therm in her hands. Bridger continued down the line.

"Jan!"

Jan issued flatly, "Ready for home."

"Come on, man, give it some feeling!" Bridger said. Jan stared at him for a moment.

The whole situation seemed awkward until he shouted, "Ready for home!" at the top of his lungs.

"Very good," Bridger said, patting him on the shoulder and continuing down the line.

A call of "Howie," was met with another reply.

"Herb!"

"Ready for home!" called the seasoned old gunner.

He stood before me and met my eyes. I became acutely aware of the pain from my wound as I struggled to stand at attention.

"Atoll!"

I blinked. I reached for my therm and held it tightly as I painstakingly yelled, "Ready for home!"

"All troops ready for home!" Jan said, stepping out of the line.

"Good to know," Bridger replied before shouting, "Get to that gunship, Special Operators! We're done here!"

I couldn't run like some of the others as we approached and boarded the second gunship. Bridger was the last to board. I sat next to a window, practically pressing my face up against it as the whining engine started up, the turbines began to whip, and the craft slowly ascended.

Fifty feet, then one hundred. Then five hundred. Even at this height, we hadn't breached the tops of some of the tallest skyscrapers, or even the Aug-Tek building itself. I watched intently as we flew past the great abandoned skyscrapers and the widespread damage to the old city. As I thought of the lives in Sardouria we had saved today, I concluded that my suffering was worth it. No one else would have to navigate through these mined streets or face defections and insurgents. The gunship glided through the air, and I saw the occasional Sardourian mop-up operation surrounding whole units of Kabat Vi. Finally, we left the borders of the massive city. While I hoped it would be my last time there, I also felt a slight tinge of wistfulness. It had been ravaged by the war and warped into an unrecognizable ecosystem of lifeless concrete and steel. Watching the great skyscrapers and buildings grow smaller behind us, I peeled my head back from the window and receded to my thoughts. No one spoke.

Undoubtedly, there would continue to be skirmishes after the city fell; I had known enough of the Insurrectionist strategy to recognize they wouldn't give up so easily. I also knew more clearly than anything else that we had dealt a heavy blow to their cause.

The curtains of this theater were descending, and maybe Iron Spires would get another chance. The opportunity to return to the peaceful existence that so many had known before the war was a tantalizing one, and I was sure it was what the people of the city deserved. It was right for them.

For myself, I wasn't so sure. I was ready to face my next assignment with the same dedication as this one, but knew that Iron Spires would remain in my thoughts for many years to come.

Acknowledgements

This project has taken a large amount of time and effort on the part of many different people. First and foremost, I want to express my gratitude towards Sarah Olson, who edited the book. Her feedback and comments were extremely helpful in bringing this story up to its current state. I also want to thank everyone else at Fox Pointe Publishing for giving me the opportunity to have a published story. Finally, I am enormously grateful to my family for supporting me during this project; my grandparents for writing advice, my parents for support on aspects of writing a book I didn't even know existed, and my sister for always being encouraging. Without them, it would not have been possible.

Photography by Ashley Mattson

About the Author

Liam Ulland-Joy is a high school student who lives in Marquette, Michigan. He began writing at an early age, going on to win a Silver National Medal and an Honorable Mention at the Scholastic Art and Writing Awards.